THE ROAD TO BALINOR

Read all the Unicorns of Balinor books:

UNICORNS OF BALINOR

THE ROAD TO BALINOR

MARY STANTON

AN
APPLE
PAPERBACK

SCHOLASTIC INC.
New York Toronto London Auckland Sydney
Mexico City New Delhi Hong Kong Buenos Aires

For Les Stanton,
A Hero All the Way.

Cover illustration by D. Craig

ISBN 0-439-06280-2

12   4 5/0

Printed in the U.S.A.   40
First Scholastic printing, May 1999

1

It was dawn in the Celestial Valley. The sky over the Eastern Ridge slowly turned pink. Silver light spilled across the wooded hills, touching the waters of the river winding through meadows and flowering trees, then spreading over the herd of sleeping unicorns.

A few unicorns stirred in their sleep. All slept peacefully. The Celestial Valley was their home, and had been since time began. Above the valley, between the clouds that drifted across the sky, was the home of the gods and goddesses who had created them. Below the valley, by way of a rocky, treacherous path known only to a few, lay the world of humans. In this world, there was Balinor, the country guarded by the celestial unicorns, and then there was the land beyond the Gap. The Gap was haunted by mists and legends. A few chosen unicorns had been down to Balinor, fewer still had crossed over

1

the Gap to Earth. But for thousands of years, after each sunrise in the Celestial Valley, all the unicorns had gathered shoulder to shoulder to form the rainbow. Then they would sing in the new day.

They wouldn't fully awaken until the sun itself peeked over the ridge. And for now, the sun was still out of sight behind the mountains. So they slept, curled horn-to-tail. Some lay back-to-back, others dozed peacefully alone under the sapphire willows that lined the banks of the Imperial River.

All of them slept but one.

Atalanta, the Dreamspeaker, was up early. She hadn't rested at all that night. Just before the sun came up, she gave up trying to rest. She trotted up the Eastern Ridge to the Watching Pool to wait for the visions she knew would come.

Atalanta was the color of the sky before moonrise, a soft blend of lavender, violet, and shadowy grays. Her mane, tail, and horn were of purest silver. She was the mate of Numinor, the Golden One, leader of the Celestial Valley herd. As the Dreamspeaker, Atalanta was the link between unicorns and the world of humans, just as twilight was the link between night and day. Atalanta, alone of all the celestial unicorns, could appear in the dreams of both humans and animals alike. And she was able to call up visions from the Watching Pool, where magic allowed Atalanta to watch events in the world of humans below.

The headwaters of the Imperial River formed

the Watching Pool. The Imperial River began as a small stream trickling from a curiously shaped stone spout in the side of the ridge. This stream flowed into a pond lined with amethyst rock, and from there into a waterfall that fed the Imperial River.

The jeweled rocks — found nowhere else in the Celestial Valley — formed a glittering violet circle, perfectly round and enormously deep. This was the Watching Pool. Atalanta stood there now, hock-deep in the velvety grass that lined the banks. Images formed there, one after the other. The visions remained for a few moments, then sank to the depths of the pool. They disappeared like snowflakes. Atalanta knew she didn't have much time to watch the visions.

She bent over the Watching Pool and touched her horn upon the water, saying, "I, Atalanta, Dreamspeaker, call forth the Princess of Balinor."

The silvery-blue water stirred clockwise, faster and faster. Small waves slapped against the amethyst rock. The waters dimpled, as if an invisible hand scattered raindrops on the surface. Then the whirlpool stilled, and an image formed in the water.

Atalanta saw a slender, bronze-haired girl twisted in pain on a hospital bed. Her legs were bandaged from knee to ankle. "Arianna!" Atalanta called. But the girl made no answer. She slept; a deep, unnatural sleep that Atalanta's dreams couldn't reach. So Atalanta had been right. Arianna had been gravely hurt.

Atalanta's purple eyes filled with grief.

The Dreamspeaker touched her horn twice more on the water. The girl in the hospital bed faded into the depths of the Watching Pool. A new vision formed.

A unicorn stallion knelt in a dark horse stall, head bowed so that his muzzle touched the ground. His coat was bronze, the same hair color as that of the girl on the hospital bed. Atalanta knew him: He was the Sunchaser, Lord of Animals in the world of humans, Bonded to Arianna, and kin to Atalanta herself. Not so long ago, Atalanta watched the Sunchaser, tall and proud down in Balinor. Now he lay wounded on the other side of the Gap. There was a bloody stump in the center of his forehead where his bronze horn once had been.

He groaned once, enduring a pain-filled sleep.

"Sunchaser!" Atalanta called.

The great unicorn raised his head. Atalanta quivered. His bronze horn was gone! A cruel white scar was the only reminder of his former glory. His dark brown eyes were dull. He dropped his head onto the stall floor and lay still. He had heard her Dreamspeaking, Atalanta was sure of it. But he no longer understood the Unicorn's language — he could no longer speak!

Two tears slid down Atalanta's cheeks and dropped into the water of the Watching Pool.

The image of the bronze unicorn sank. Atalanta held her breath, reluctant to see what she had to see next. She shook herself all over, scattering a flowery scent through the cool air. The Sunchaser, greatest of those unicorns who roamed the world of humans, lay broken beyond the reach of the Celestial Valley herd; Arianna, the lost Princess of Balinor, endured the pain of mangled legs, not knowing who she really was. Atalanta couldn't bear the horror of what would next appear in the Watching Pool.

But she had to know: Did Entia, the evil Shifter, know where the Princess and her wounded unicorn were hidden? And if he did, what terrible vengeance would the Shifter seek?

2

Arianna Langley opened her eyes to the dull green of the hospital ceiling. As dim as it was, the light made her head hurt. Her stomach was empty and her throat was raw, as if she'd thrown up after being sick.

"Feelin' better, honey?"

Ari turned her head. This was a mistake. The room swayed, and her stomach lurched.

"The anesthetic made you sicker 'n a *dog*."

A fat woman sat in a chair next to her bed. Large. Large and familiar. Ari narrowed her eyes, trying to focus.

"It's Ann," the large lady said helpfully. "The doc said you might have a little trouble rememberin'." Ann was dressed in blue jeans, a red sweatshirt, and a tentlike denim jacket. A little embroidered horse galloped across the jacket's breast pocket. Ari's head swam. It wasn't a horse — it was a unicorn.

Ann chuckled nervously. "You recall any-thing at all, honey?"

"My name. I remember my name." She rested her head against the pillows. Her stomach was feeling better now. "Arianna Langley."

Ann didn't say anything for a moment. Then, "Right you are, sweetie."

"What happened to me?" She raised herself off the pillow, which was harder than it should have been. It was as if she was pushing a dead weight. She looked down at her legs. Both of them were wrapped in casts. "What happened to me!" she gasped.

Ann patted Ari's hand. "You just rest a little bit now. I'm goin' to find the doctor and she'll explain the whole thing. It's just lucky you weren't hurt worse, that's all."

Ari fell back onto her pillow. A confusion of memories hit her. A tunnel. The smell of dead and dying things. The sound of black flies buzzing. A great bronze four-legged creature plunging in front of her. "Chase!" she shouted suddenly. "Where's Chase?"

"Shush-shush-shush!" Ann's face was pale. She looked nervously over her shoulder. "Chase is fine," Ann said. "It's a miracle, really. I thought that poor . . . uh . . . horse was a goner. But he came out of the accident with a big ol' bump on his head, and that was about it."

"Chase is a horse?" Ari frowned. "That's

7

not . . ." She trailed off. Her head hurt. And she couldn't remember a thing about who she was or where she'd been. Just her name . . . and the tunnel. She turned her head so that Ann wouldn't see the tears. Her hair lay spread across the pillow, the bronze gleaming dully in the indirect light. There was something familiar about the color of her hair. That color was hers, but it also belonged to someone, something else. Chase! The Chaser! "Chase?" she asked. "Chase is my horse?"

"Horse," Ann said firmly. "He's right at home, in his stall at Glacier River Farm." Ann heaved herself to her feet. Her eyes were small and brown. She gave Ari a thoughtful look. "He's gonna be just fine except for that wound on his forehead. We had the vet take care of that."

"Good," Ari said doubtfully. "A vet is taking care of him."

"Best vet we've got!" Ann said cheerfully.

"What happened to him?" Ari asked.

"Oh, jeez." Ann ran a chubby palm through her scant brown hair. "Don't you fret. I'll go get the doc. Now that you're awake, we can talk about gettin' you back home, too."

But the doctor didn't hold out much hope for going home, at least not right away. She was a tall, neat woman with blond hair pulled into a tight bun at the back of her neck. Her hands were cool and sympathetic on Ari's aching head. She smiled at

8

Ari, took her pulse, and gazed intently into her eyes with a penlight. "Can you sleep a little now, Ari?" Her voice was kind.

"Yes," Ari said.

"Are you in a lot of pain?"

"No," Ari lied.

"Hmm." She bent over and examined the casts on both legs, one after the other. "I'm going to give you a mild painkiller, okay? Then sleep if you can. Sleep's the best thing for you right now." The doctor took a small syringe from a collection of instruments on the bedside table and slipped the shot into Ari's arm. The needle was so thin Ari hardly felt the sting at all. In a few moments, the terrible ache in her head and legs receded, and Ari sank gratefully back onto the pillows. She could sleep now. And suddenly, that's all she wanted to do. Sleep.

The doctor drew the curtains around the hospital bed and left Ari alone. Sleep began to drift around her. "Retrograde amnesia," Ari heard the doctor say to Ann. "I'm surprised she even remembers her name. She seems to recall a few things about her life before the accident. But it's bits and pieces, nothing more. It's going to take a while. And I have to tell you, Mrs. Langley, her entire memory may never come back."

"She's all right in other ways, though?" Ari heard Ann ask.

"Except for the two compound fractures of the lower legs." The doctor's voice was dry. "She's going to take a while to heal."

"Will she be able to walk?"

"I don't know." The doctor hesitated. "There'll be scars, of course. And perhaps a permanent limp. But your foster daughter's very fortunate, ma'am. She's not going to lose either leg. Not if I can help it."

Lose my legs! Ari thought. *No! NO!*

Sleep came like a wave of dark water. She sank beneath it gratefully. She didn't want to think. Not of the past, which she couldn't recall anyway, or of the future, which she feared.

Arianna woke up. The slant of the sun through the window told her it was late afternoon. The pain in her legs was dull, constant but bearable. She made herself calm and tried to think.

She was Ari Langley. She was thirteen. She'd been in the hospital for several days, maybe more. There'd been an operation on her legs.

She had a horse named Chase. She had a foster mother named Ann. And she must have a home, this place called Glacier River Farm that Ann had mentioned.

None of this seemed right. But Ann had said it was right. And Ann was her foster mother. That was what the doctor had said.

But who was Ari Langley? What had happened to her?

She didn't know. She couldn't recall. There had been some sort of tunnel, hadn't there? And an accident. But even those memories, fragmented as they were, didn't tell her who she was or why she was here. Or where she was going. Panic hit her. She was so alone! She didn't remember anyone!

"Calm down," she murmured to herself. "Keep calm." She clenched her hands and relaxed, deliberately. She would take things one at a time.

Okay. She was in a hospital bed. The sheets were clean and smelled of starch. A nightstand was on her left, a plastic chair on her right. The room was — how large was the room? And there was a window. So she could see out. Perhaps discover what this strange place was.

3

Atalanta saw Arianna lie back in the hospital bed and drop into a deep sleep from the drug she had been given by the doctor. Then the image disappeared as fast as a candle blows out. Atalanta reared in distress. The princess didn't know who she was! She barely remembered the Sunchaser! And now the visions in the Watching Pool were failing. Was this the Shifter's work? His evil magic had never before worked in the haven of the Celestial Valley. Only in Balinor. And the celestial unicorns had helped send Arianna and her unicorn to safety on the other side of the Gap — where they should have been safe from the demon Shifter's work.

Driven by fear, Atalanta struck the water in the Watching Pool three times with her silver horn. She had to find out! She chanted the words to the water over and over again until finally she saw Ari, sitting upright in a wheelchair.

Atalanta wasn't sure how much time had passed on the other side of the Gap. It could have been minutes — it could have been days. Arianna was talking to Anale, one of the two servants Atalanta had commanded to attend Arianna on the other side of the Gap. She heard Arianna call her Ann.

Atalanta calmed down. Perhaps things were going to be all right after all.

Suddenly, unbidden, the waters of the Watching Pool darkened to black. A tiny whirlwind appeared at the bottom of the pool. It rose swiftly through the water and burst into the air. It was a vision of black flies! Thousands of them, spinning in a vicious vortex of spite and hate. Atalanta forced herself to stand. Black flies were terrifying to her and to her kind. There had been times — too many times! — when the evil made by the Shifter turned into swarms of stinging flies, filling the unicorns' ears and sensitive noses, blinding their eyes.

For now, the swarm was only an image. No actual harm could come to the herd through the Watching Pool. Just the terror of the visions.

The flies filled the water from edge to edge, then disappeared.

Atalanta took a deep breath and looked into the waters.

She saw an iron gate, spikes reaching to a black and threatening sky. An ominous smear of dark, dirty clouds drifted behind the gate. The smear billowed and shrank, then shifted into a towering pillar of fire and darkness. Sickly yellow-green light wheeled in the center of the pillar. Gradually, the light resolved itself into a lidless eye. There was a face and form behind the Eye, but yellow-green clouds of smoke obscured them. All Atalanta could see was the lidless socket, the pupil blazing red.

The Eye of Entia, the Shifter!

The Shifter was enemy of all humans and animals in the worlds above and below the Celestial Valley. A demon — or worse! — whom no living being had ever seen. A ghastly presence that could shift, change shape, look like friend or foe, and no one could tell the difference. The only safety humans and unicorns had against the Shifter was that he couldn't hold a shape — any shape — for more than a few hours.

No one really knew the nature of the Shifter's Eye. Some said it was a part of the ghoul himself, split off in the time before animals could speak. Others said it was a grisly servant, created by the Shifter to spy on all those that he considered his enemies.

The area around the demon-red pupil was a wounded white, filled with red veins engorged with blood. The fiery pupil rolled in the socket, searching for prey.

And then the voice of the Shifter called for the Princess of Balinor. *"Arianna!"*

It was a huge, hollow voice, with the timbre of dull iron. It filled Atalanta with horror.

"Arianna!"

The Eye rolled as the voice called. Searching, while its Master distracted Atalanta with his calling.

The Shifter's voice echoed a third time, filled with a horrible coaxing.

"Arianna!"

Atalanta shivered. She struck the water sharply, one decisive blow that made the waters part and foam over the Shifter's terrible form. The dreadful Eye winked out. The Shifter's voice sounded farther and farther away, still calling for the bronze-haired girl. Finally, the voice was gone. The waters of the Watching Pool shone clear.

But now Atalanta knew why she hadn't slept last night. She had thought the Princess would be safe in the place where the unicorns had sent her. Instead, the Princess and the Sunchaser were in danger worse than they had been before. They were both wounded. They were separated. And the Shifter's Eye searched on. Atalanta knew that what the Shifter wanted, the Shifter got. He never gave up.

The events in the Pool meant sad news for Numinor, the Golden One, King of the Celestial Valley herd.

Atalanta left the banks of the Imperial River and walked through the meadow to the Crystal

Arch. This was the bridge between the Celestial Valley and the worlds above and below. This was where the rainbow was formed each morning, and where the unicorns sang in the new day.

Hooves whispering in the scented grass, the unicorns lined up under the Crystal Arch, ears alert, tails high, manes waving gently in the light breeze. Their horns shone and their glossy coats gleamed in the tender light of the fresh morning. There were hundreds of unicorns, one for each of all the colors of the Celestial Valley and all the worlds above and below it. Each unicorn made a separate part of the rainbow, from the violet Atalanta herself to the crimson Rednal of the Fiery Coals.

By custom, they faced the east. They waited for Numinor, the Golden One, lead stallion of the Celestial Valley herd. And as the sun's rim cleared the top of the Eastern Ridge, the stallion himself came down the mountain.

Numinor was the color of the sun at high noon. His shining mane fell to his knees. His tail floated like a golden banner. At the base of his golden horn, a diamond sparkled brighter than the sun itself. This jewel — like the jewels at the base of all the unicorns' horns in every part of the Celestial Valley — held a unicorn's personal magic.

Numinor trotted powerfully over the rocks and brush that lay on the side of his mountain. He halted in front of the rainbow ranks and arched his neck.

"I greet the rainbow," Numinor said, his voice like a great bronze bell.

"We welcome the sun," the unicorns said in response.

And then they all sang the first part of the Ceremony to Greet the Sun, as they had from the beginning of time:

"Red and yellow, orange and green
Purple, silver, and blue
The rainbow we make defends those we guard
In Balinor's cities and fields."

And Numinor asked, "When will we cross the Crystal Arch, to walk to the earth below?"

"When the dwellers of Balinor need us!" the unicorns responded.

Then they turned to the rising sun, toward the One Who Rules humans and animals alike. They pledged in a mighty chorus: *"We guard life! We guard freedom! We guard peace!"*

The Ceremony to Greet the Sun was over. Most of the unicorns dropped their heads abruptly to the grass and began to eat, which was their favorite occupation unless there was work to be done below. Numinor nodded to Atalanta and she approached. It was time to talk.

"Any news?" Numinor's eyes were wise and kind.

"It's very bad," Atalanta said. "With the help

of the resistance movement in Balinor, we sent the Princess through the Gap to live in safety at Glacier River Farm. The Sunchaser went with her, of course. But things went wrong. She's hurt. And there's worse."

Numinor's golden eyes widened. There was alarm in his deep voice. "Worse than the Princess's injury? How seriously is she wounded?"

"I can't tell. Not from here. She's alive. But her legs have been broken."

"And the Sunchaser? He is not . . . dead?"

"He has lost his horn, and the jewel that holds his magic. He has lost the ability to speak. I called to him, Numinor. I know he heard me. But he didn't understand me! What's worse, the two of them are separated. She is in a human place, with Anale and Franc to guard her, as we planned. "

"And Sunchaser?"

"He's at the farm. As we had hoped. But he is lost to us."

Numinor closed his eyes and breathed out hard, as a stallion will when he is angry. For a moment, he said nothing. Then he said, "The Sacred Bond between the Princess and Sunchaser? Does the loss of his horn and jewel mean he is deaf and dumb to the Princess, too?"

Atalanta sighed. "I don't know. A great deal depends upon Arianna herself. We've never sent a Bonded Pair through the Gap before, of course. And the Princess and the Sunchaser are more than just a

Bonded Pair, they are the source of bonds between all humans and animals in Balinor."

Numinor tapped his foreleg impatiently. He knew this. What he didn't know was what the consequences would be if the bond between the Sunchaser and the Princess was broken. For generations, the Royal Family of Balinor had dedicated the firstborn Princess to a unicorn from the Celestial Valley. The bond between the two was a unique magic, a magic that created the friendships between humans and animals in the world below.

"Atalanta? Do you know what may happen?"

She shook her head. "I'm worried, Numinor. The very nature of the Shifter's magic seems to be changing! He — or something — snatched the vision right from the waters of the pool! It took me many moments to get it back."

"But you did."

"I did. But I was *not* able to see what happened to Arianna for far too long a time."

"But when you were able to see again?"

"She seemed to be fine." A line of worry appeared between her eyes. "I think."

"Entia the Shifter? Our enemy?" Numinor half reared, his forelegs striking the air as if to strike at the Shifter himself. "Does he dare to attack our own?"

"He has sent his Eye to look for them. As far as I can see, he has not found them yet. I doubt he knows how to get through the Gap. But if we discovered how to get Arianna and the Sunchaser to Glacier River Farm, it won't be long before he figures it out, too."

Atalanta's mane drifted in front of her face, obscuring her violet eyes for a moment. "Who knows what will happen then? Our magic is limited on the other side of the Gap. I thought his evil was, too. Now I am not so sure. The loss of visions from the Watching Pool is not natural. And I have no idea what happened to Arianna between the time I saw her fall asleep in the hospital and when I saw her in the wheelchair. But I do know this: Without Arianna and the Sunchaser, the animals in Balinor will begin to lose their ability to speak. And when that happens, there will be chaos. If the bullocks can't be asked to pull the plow, there will be no crops, and eventually no food. If the Balinor unicorns can't be told where to carry their riders, the army won't be able to fight! Balinor will be in the Shifter's power.

"And then . . ." Atalanta turned to face the sun. Her horn gleamed with a hot, pure light. "The waters of the Watching Pool will go dark. Humans and animals alike will be forced into slavery to serve the Shifter's will. Then, Numinor, the Imperial River will dry up, and the Celestial Valley will wither. The Shifter will attack us here. And if we lose . . ." Her voice trailed away.

Atalanta's deep purple gaze swept the lovely valley. The sapphire willow trees were in full flower.

The meadow was thick and green. Two unicorn colts skipped in the sunshine and sang. She said, so softly that Numinor could barely hear her, "All this will be lost."

The great stallion looked toward the sun. His voice was grim. "It's what the Shifter wants, Atalanta. Chaos. The animals of Balinor used as slaves and worse. So he can rule totally and without opposition. He has already kidnapped the King and Queen. Hidden the Princes. All this before we could act. We thought that sending Arianna and the Sunchaser through the Gap would at least ensure that the humans and animals of Balinor could still speak together. If they cannot, if the two races cannot communicate, there is no way the Shifter can be overthrown."

Atalanta stood close to Numinor. He smelled of fresh grass and clear water. The terrible Eye was gone, but it seemed to her that a faint scent of dead and dying things still drifted in the air. "You know the law, Numinor. I cannot cross into the Gap. Not unless Arianna and the Sunchaser summon me. I can only appear to her in dreams. That's all. If for some reason she cannot bond with the Sunchaser, we are in terrible trouble indeed."

"There must be something we can do, Atalanta."

The Dreamspeaker bowed her head in thought. "There may be one thing, at least. If I can

21

find the Sunchaser's jewel and get it to him, it may help him, and Ari, too. The jewel is a crucial part of the bonding, Numinor."

"I know that," the stallion said testily. "But where is it? And how will you get to the Sunchaser? And how will he know what to do with it when he does have it?"

"Leave that to me."

"I have left it to you. I've left it to you and look what's happened!"

Atalanta looked at him, a long, level look. "Do you wish to quarrel, Numinor? After all these years together? It's to the Shifter's advantage to have us at each other's throats."

"You're right. I'm sorry. But this . . . our whole way of life! It could disappear in war!"

"I will do all I can do. But I have to act now. The Shifter may have thought of it himself. If he has . . ." She closed her eyes. "I won't think about it. Not now. Leave me, Numinor. I have work to do. I have to send someone to help them."

4

Ari jerked from her deep sleep. Was that a sound of bells? She blinked. Time had passed. She didn't know how much. Suddenly, she knew without a doubt there was someone else in the hospital room with her.

Instinctively, she grabbed for the heaviest weapon she could find — her water pitcher. She held her breath. Her hand tightened on the pitcher. Whatever this danger was, she was ready.

A dog trotted around the side of the hospital bed and thrust its cold nose under her hand. Ari breathed out in relief. The dog was friendly. She could tell that right away. It was a male collie with a magnificent gold-and-black coat. The ruff around his neck was creamy white. His head was elegantly narrow, and his ears were up. A white blaze ran down the middle of his tawny nose.

Ari ran her fingers gently over his head, then snuggled them deep in his ruff. If he had a collar, she might be able to find his owner. Yes, there it was, a thin chain wound deep in the fur. Was that what had made the chiming sound? She fumbled for a minute, then tugged it free.

A necklace, not a collar! She held it up. The chain was made of a fine silver and gold metal. Each link in the chain was a curiously twisted spiral. A ruby-colored jewel hung at the end, as large as her thumb. The late afternoon sun struck crimson lights from the jewel. "Well!" Ari said. "Your owner must miss this!"

The dog barked and pawed urgently at her hand.

"Shall I keep it for you? It might get lost if you have it. And we'll give it back when we find your master."

He panted happily at her, then licked her wrist with his pink tongue. Ari slipped the chain over her neck. The ruby nestled against her chest. It was warm, perhaps from being snuggled in the dog's fur.

"Who are you?" Ari asked softly. "And what are you doing here?"

The dog nudged her hand with his head. Suddenly, he turned to face the door to her room. A low rumbling began in his throat. It rose to a growl, then a snarl. The door swung inward, and a nurse Ari didn't know walked into the room. He was pushing a wheelchair. He stopped at the sight of the menacing dog.

"Wow," he said. "Hey." He lifted both hands,

24

either to keep the dog away, or to show that he didn't mean any harm. "Don't make any sudden moves, Miss Langley. You just keep calm." He edged sideways into the room. The dog swung his head as the nurse came closer. The snarls increased. "Now look, Miss Langley. I know you can't get out of bed, but you can cover your head and chest with the pillows, okay? I'm gonna have to call Security. I can't handle a dog this big by myself. But you're going to be all right. Just stay calm."

"I am calm," Ari said. "I'm just fine." She tapped the dog lightly on the head. "Easy, boy. Easy."

The growls stopped. The collie turned and looked up at her, as if to say, *Are you sure this is okay?*

"I'm sure," Ari said. "Lie down, boy."

The big dog lay down with a thump.

"It's *your* dog?" the nurse said in astonishment. His face turned red with embarrassment and anger. "You can't keep a dog in here!"

The door behind him banged open. Two uniformed men rushed in. Behind them were Ann and a thin man with a worried face and a long brown mustache. The collie leaped to his feet, then backed protectively against the bed, staying between Ari and the others.

"Linc! Lincoln!" Ann said. "There he is! Come here, boy. Come *here*! Frank! Do something!"

The worried-looking man dropped to one knee and began to chirp, "Here, Lincoln. Good doggie. Good doggie."

The dog turned to Ari, ignoring them all. There was a question in his deep brown eyes. Ari twined one hand deep in his ruff.

"He jumped in the car when we left the farm," Ann explained to the security guard. "Then he jumped out when we got to the hospital and ran off. I don't know how he knew Ari was here. He's always been her dog, and none of us can do a thing with him. Lincoln!" she added despairingly. "Come HERE!"

"Lincoln," Ari said. "Is that your name?"

He barked. Ari's hand went to the neck of her hospital gown. The ruby lay warm beneath her hand. If the necklace belonged to the collie's owner — then the jewel was hers?

"You don't remember Lincoln?" Ann burst into tears. Frank patted her awkwardly on the back. "Oh, Ari. Oh, Ari!" Ann sobbed.

"I don't care if it belongs to the President of the United States, that dog has got to go," the nurse said. "Here, you two guys are with Security, right? Take him out of here."

Lincoln growled. He rolled his upper lip back, showing his sharp white teeth. The two security men exchanged a nervous look. One of them cleared his throat. "Ah," he said, "I don't think this-here is in my job description. I don't think it is. No-sir."

"It doesn't matter," Ann said impatiently. She wiped her nose with the back of her hand and

26

sniffed. "Ari's coming home with us now, anyway, and the dog goes wherever she goes."

"You know the doctors don't think she's ready to go home," the nurse said in a fussy way. "If you two were responsible foster parents, you'd keep her right here. Where she belongs."

"Responsible foster parents don't run up hospital bills they can't pay," Ann said tartly. "And we've made some arrangements. A friend of ours suddenly showed up this afternoon, and she's going to stay with Ari as long as we need her. She's a medical person, a veterinarian. Her name is Dr. Bohnes. You remember Dr. Bohnes, Ari?"

Ari didn't. She shook her head. All at once, an image of a short, stocky old lady with bright blue eyes and white hair popped into her head. As if someone or something had sent the image to her!

"Well, you will," Ann said in a positive way. "She's a very old friend of yours, milady, I mean Ari." She turned back to the nurse. "So you see? We can take Ari home now. Dr. Bohnes has been given all the instructions needed for her therapy. She'll get the best care we can give her. Come on, Ari. Let's get you *home.*"

Ari allowed herself to be helped into the wheelchair. Ann draped a light jacket over her shoulders and a cotton throw over her knees. Then the nurse pushed the wheelchair down the long corridor and out into the sunshine. Lincoln walked gravely by her side.

Free of the hospital at last! Ari blinked in the bright light, at the cars in the parking lot, a plane flying overhead, the smell of gasoline, the crowds of people. Ann explained everything Ari saw. Each time Ari asked and asked again, she felt more desperate. None of this was familiar. None of this was *home*. But she had no idea of what *would* be home. Ann and Frank helped her into the van. They were on their way to Glacier River Farm.

Ari kept a tight hand on Lincoln's ruff and tried to fight her fear.

Frank lifted Ari onto the backseat and folded the wheelchair down to store it. Ari held on to the overhead strap and gazed out the window all the way to the farm. They passed quickly through the city and out onto a huge road that seemed to end at the sky. "The Thruway," Ann explained. "The farm is only twenty minutes from here. Do you remember yet?"

Ari remembered nothing. She held on to the collie as the van went down an exit ramp and turned onto a small deserted road. They passed fields of corn and purple-green alfalfa. Finally, they came to a long stretch of white three-board fence. A sign read GLACIER RIVER FARM, with an arrow pointing away from them toward the east.

Frank turned into a winding driveway made of gravel and stone, and they bumped along toward a large gray farmhouse standing on the crest of the hill. Long gray barns with green roofs spilled down the hillside. Ari could see horses in the pastures, grazing quietly under the sun.

"You'll want to see Chase first, I expect." Ann turned and looked at Ari over the passenger headrest.

CHASE! Ari's heart leaped at the name. Her hand tightened on Linc's ruff. He whined in sympathy. The van bumped to a stop in front of the largest barn. Ari waited patiently while Frank carefully set the wheelchair up on the gravel drive. Then he reached into the van and hoisted Ari into the chair with a grunt of effort.

"Watch her legs, Frank," Ann fussed. "Take it easy, now. And don't push her too fast!"

Frank rolled the chair into the barn. Ari took a deep breath: She loved the barn at once. There was the scent of horses, straw, and the spicy odor of sun-cured hay. Stalls lined the broad gravel aisle. Most of them were empty, but a few curious horses poked their heads over the half doors and watched the little procession roll past. Lincoln trotted beside Ari, his head up, ears tuliped forward in eager attention. His eyes brightened. And as they came to the end of the long aisle, to a large box stall in the corner, he gave a welcoming bark.

Frank rolled the wheelchair to a stop and stepped back. Ari couldn't see anything in the gloom at first. Her heart beating fast, she rolled herself forward, then pushed the half door to the stall aside. It rolled back and daylight flooded in. A great shape lay curled in the corner. The head turned as

29

she rolled farther into the stall, and then the animal got to his feet.

It was a stallion. The light gleamed on his bronze coat. His chest and quarters were heavily muscled, his withers well-shaped. But it was his head and eyes that were the most beautiful to Ari. His forehead was broad, the muzzle well-shaped, with delicately flared nostrils. As he stepped forward, she looked deep into his eyes, large, brown, and full of sorrow.

"Chase," she whispered. "You are Chase. I . . . Ann!" She gasped and bit short a scream. The light hit a great wound in his forehead. She could see the stitches holding the gouge shut.

"The accident," Ann said gloomily. "Hadn't been for Dr. Bohnes, we might have lost him."

"Might have lost Ari as well," a tart voice snapped.

"Oh, Dr. Bohnes." Frank gave his mustache a nervous tug and backed away respectfully. The vet marched into the stall and put her hand on Ari's shoulder. She was small, but sturdily built, with snow-white hair and bright blue eyes. She was wearing high rubber boots, a stethoscope swinging from her neck.

Ari half turned in her wheelchair, reluctant to take her eyes from the stallion. If she gazed at him long enough, if she could touch him . . .

"Do you remember anything?" Dr. Bohnes asked softly.

"I know his name," Ari said sadly. "And that's all. He is mine, isn't he?"

"Till the end of time." Dr. Bohnes clapped her hands together with a competent air. Her sharp blue eyes traveled over Ari's face. "Humph! They didn't feed you too well in that place, I see."

"Please!" Ari said. She stretched her hands out to the stallion. He stepped forward delicately, as if treading on fragile ground. He bent his head and breathed into her hair. "Chase!" Ari cried. She wound her arms around his neck, as far as she could reach. She laid her cheek against his warm chest. She could feel the mighty heart, slow and steady, and his even breathing.

"Do you remember . . . anything?" Dr. Bohnes asked softly.

"I've lost something!" Ari cried. "That's all I know. But I don't know what it is!"

Dr. Bohnes patted her back in brisk sympathy. "I'll tell you what, young lady. We'll get to work on those legs of yours. And I know just what will help strengthen them."

"Riding?" Ann said, her voice alight with satisfaction.

"Riding," Dr. Bohnes confirmed. "As soon as we get you on your feet, my dear, we'll get you on your horse. And as soon as we get you on your horse . . ." The three adults exchanged glances.

"Yes?" Ari prompted. She kept her hand on

31

the stallion's side, as if to make sure they wouldn't be parted again.

"Well. We'll see."

"How soon?" Ari asked. Her eyes met the stallion's, and she smiled. "How soon before I ride?"

Dr. Bohnes screwed up her face. It looked like a potato. "How soon? That, my dear, depends on you. And on how much pain you want to put up with."

Ari set her jaw. "As much as I have to," she said. "I used to ride him? Every day?"

"Never apart," Frank said sadly. He chewed his mustache with a melancholy air. "Well, you slept in the palace, I mean — in the house, of course. Not in his stall. But still!"

"We won't be apart for long," Ari promised. She raised her hands to his face. He bent his head further so that she could examine the wound on his forehead. Whatever had happened, it had been a terrible blow. The stitches had healed well, but the skin was soft over a depression right in the middle of his forehead. She remembered something: Scars like this one healed white. She closed her eyes so that the others wouldn't see the tears. Why could she remember things like this, and nothing about her own past? She felt his breath on her cheek. It was warm and smelled of grass. She looked into his eyes, and he gazed back, his own eyes searching hers.

Horses didn't look directly at humans. No animal did. Ari knew that, just the way she knew how to pull on a pair of jeans or wear a T-shirt. "Dr. Bohnes," Ari said after a moment. "The accident . . . both of us were in it?"

"That's right," Dr. Bohnes said.

"It was a car accident?"

"We don't talk about it," Ann said. "It doesn't do to talk about it. It was terrible. Terrible."

"I just wanted to know — did Chase forget, as I did? Has he lost his memory?" She rubbed her eyes. She was tired. So tired! Not much was making sense right now. "I know that's a silly question, in a way. How would you know if a horse lost his memory? But I can't help feeling that — I don't know. That he's trying to tell me something."

"Perhaps he is," Dr. Bohnes agreed. "The coming weeks will tell, won't they?" She put her hand on Ari's shoulder. "This one needs sleep, Anale. She's practically falling out of her chair. Let's get her up to bed."

"Anale," Ari said drowsily. "Anale. I knew someone by that name, once."

"You will again, milady," Ann said, tucking the blanket around her knees. Frank began to push the wheelchair down the barn aisle.

Ari could barely keep her eyes open. "Chase," she whispered. "Chase."

The stallion whinnied, a loud, trumpeting call that jerked her back from the shores of sleep. "I'll be back soon, Chase," she said. "I promise."

5

The sun sank below the Western Ridge of the Celestial Valley. A few stars shone at the edge of the twilight sky. Atalanta backed away from the Watching Pool. She was disturbed by what she'd seen. No. She was afraid. Arianna had no memory of who she was. Chase was deaf to his Bonded Mistress. And there was the dog. What was she going to do about the dog?

The Imperial River reflected the stars and the line of rainbow-shower trees that grew at the north side of the Watching Pool, but tonight the waters would not reflect the moon. This was the first night of the Shifter's Moon, when the Silver Traveler's Dark Side faced the Celestial Valley. For four nights in a row, no magic would work at all.

The Dreamspeaker cantered up the hillside. There would be no sleep again for her tonight, nor for any of the Celestial Valley herd. On Dark Side nights, the unicorns stayed awake. Mares with colts and fillies took shelter on the lee side of the valley, out of the evening wind. The others, mares and stallions alike, were supposed to pace the valley in a guardian circle, alert for sights or sounds of the Shifter's forces. There had never been an invasion of the Celestial Valley, not within Atalanta's memory. So the Ritual of the Shifter's Moon had become an excuse for staying up all night, singing, dancing, and telling stories and tales unicorns loved to hear.

It was different tonight. Because of what Atalanta had just seen, the Ritual of the Shifter's Moon was a grim necessity.

Atalanta jumped gracefully over a log, then picked her way through a fall of rocks to the place where the brood mares stood with their young. She came to a halt on an outcrop of rock. Just below her, the unicorns cropped grass and exchanged gossip. The colts and fillies jumped and rolled, excited to be up this late. Nobody, Atalanta thought sadly, had a thought of war. Only Ash, a silver-gray unicorn close to Atalanta's own color, and a leader in the Rainbow Army, knew anything at all about fighting. Ash was practicing attack. But then, Ash spent all of his free time practicing fighting, because he liked the exercise. He dove forward, forelegs extended, head down, ears flattened against his skull. His steel-gray horn pierced the night air. This movement was called the "Otter," after the sleek river creature. Then Ash darted sideways, head moving back and forth, back and forth, snapping his teeth. This was called the "Snake." Atalanta watched him for a few moments. Then she tapped her foreleg on the rock shelf.

"Friends!" she called. Her voice was low and sweet. But somehow, the call attracted the attention of the entire herd. In silence, they gathered in front of her, the rainbow colors of their coats invisible in the dim light thrown by the stars. "Friends! You must guard in pairs tonight. And tell me if you find any of these things in our valley:

"A smell of dead and dying things. This is an odor like none you've encountered before. Once you smell it, you will not mistake it.

"The sight of a black unicorn, or one with eyes of fire.

"Any human or animal unknown to us." She paused for a long moment. "Especially a dog."

"A dog, Dreamspeaker?" Rednal, the crimson unicorn, spoke. "But I thought . . . we had heard that the Princess has the Sunchaser's jewel, and that the jewel was brought to her by —"

"Be quiet!" Atalanta said, not quite angry, but close. "There are ears and eyes abroad tonight that are no friends of ours. You will not speak, or guess at what events are occurring in the world below, in Balinor, or on the other side of the Gap. We can't take the chance that it will give the enemy information that he could use. Just remember that the

36

Shifter can take the form of anything. Anything at all."

"We know that, Dreamspeaker," Rednal said cheerfully. "But even Entia himself can't hold the shape of another for very long. So if we, say, stare at a tree for more than a few minutes, and it turns into, um . . . alfalfa, we'll know immediately . . ."

"To eat it!" another unicorn called out. "Alfalfa's my favorite food!"

There were some giggles from the herd. Atalanta frowned to herself. How would they react to what she had just learned? "The nature of magic changes," she said. "We no longer know how long the Shifter can maintain a shape that is not his own. Now, I'd like three or four of you to take the colts and fillies below. Down to the windbreak by the river."

"But, Dreamspeaker." A portly mare with a very young colt by her side spoke up in protest. The colt's horn was barely the length of Atalanta's hoof, which meant he wasn't more than a few days old. "We were all going to tell stories tonight. It will be the first time for my young one here."

"Please," Atalanta said. The word was mild, but her tone wasn't. Several of the unicorns exchanged significant looks. They were a little afraid of the Dreamspeaker. There had been rumors that she went beyond the usual use of magic to . . . what, no one really knew.

There wasn't any more discussion. Two

mares herded the colts and fillies into a small circle and led them out of the grove. Atalanta waited until she was sure they couldn't hear her. Then, since there was no way to soften her news, she said it straight out.

"I did not send the dog to Arianna. I did not find the jewel." A soft breeze picked up her forelock and stirred her mane. "I don't know who did. There is other magic abroad in Balinor and beyond the Gap. I don't know where this magic is from."

"But what shall we do?" Rednal was bewildered.

"We wait. She will heal, in time. And as she does, I will send her dreams. I can do no more. Except one thing. I can hope. I shall hope. I hope that Arianna remembers who and what she is. And that she puts the Sunchaser's jewel to its proper use."

6

The first month at Glacier River Farm, Ari was confined to her room. She slept a lot, her dreams frequent and puzzling. She had no idea what they meant.

She lived for the mornings. Each morning, Frank brought Chase out to pasture and stopped beneath her window. She waved and called to him, fighting the intense longing to be up and with him. Her legs wouldn't heal fast enough. It seemed to take forever.

"You're coming along quite nicely," Dr. Bohnes said. It was a fresh summer morning. Ari's window was open. The smell of new-mown grass drifted into her room. Six weeks before, she had come home from the hospital. Her days had been an endless round of doctor's visits, and X rays, and casts.

She was tired of it all. And even the memory of the tunnel had faded.

Dr. Bohnes picked up another gob of salve from the jar and dug her fingers into Ari's right calf.

Ari winced, but she didn't cry out. The massage therapy worked. She'd walked outside on the lawn every day this week, hardly using the crutches at all. "But when can I ride Chase?"

Dr. Bohnes's old fingers were strong. She worked the salve all the way down to Ari's ankle, then took an elastic bandage and wrapped her leg all the way to the knee. "Get up," she said.

Ari swung her legs over the side of the bed. Linc was asleep on the floor and she nudged him gently with her toe. He opened one eye and yawned, then rolled out of the way. She stood up, determined not to use the cane. Pain slammed her right leg like a hot iron brand. She bit her lip and shifted her weight to her left side. That at least was only an ache. "It's fine," she said with a gasp. "Just fine."

"Hmph." Dr. Bohnes drew her eyebrows together in a skeptical way. "You're going down to dinner tonight? With Frank and Ann?"

"Yes."

"You ask your foster parents about riding Chase."

"They'll want to know if it's okay with you."

"It's okay with me."

"Then is there a problem? Chase is mine, isn't he." She didn't say this as a question. She'd asked questions for two months. Where are my real parents? How long have I lived here? Where did I live before? Why are my dreams so weird? And Dr. Bohnes didn't have any answers. None that Ari believed, at any rate. But Ari didn't have to ask who owned Chase, she *knew* it: Chase was hers. Forever.

Dr. Bohnes narrowed her eyes. They were a sharp, clear blue. Ari thought they saw everything. "Your memory any better?"

Ari shook her head.

"Well. You'll remember how to ride. It's like breathing, to somebody like you, anyhow."

"I rode? Was I . . ." Ari was shy of this particular question, but she had to ask. "Was I any good?"

"You were very good." Dr. Bohnes sniffed disapprovingly. Ari blushed. Being conceited was the worst crime ever in Dr. Bohnes's mind. Um . . . no, Ari thought. The second worst crime. Abusing an animal was worse. Dr. Bohnes rapped her knuckles with the stethoscope. "Are you listening to me? I'm giving you your riding program. Don't blink those big blue eyes at me, miss. I know how excited you are. Now. You ride twenty minutes *once* a day for a week. Hot baths every day and more massage. Then you can ride twenty minutes *twice* a day for a week. All at the walk. Then divide the time in the saddle between the walk and the trot. We'll extend the time, twenty minutes at a time, until you're up to an hour. Once you're up to an hour, you can try cantering. No jumping for a month."

"No jumping for a month," Ari concluded at dinner. She was so excited, she hardly noticed what she was eating. "So if it's fine with Dr. Bohnes, it's fine with you?"

Ann poked her fork into her mashed potatoes. "You tell her, Frank."

"Me!" Frank twisted his mustache. Then he ran his hands through his hair. He'd been eating peas, and one of them was stuck in his thin, wispy beard. "Why me?"

Ann put her fork down and glared at him. "Because *I'm* not gonna do it."

"Tell me what?" Ari asked.

"There's a problem with Chase."

Ari's heart went cold in her chest. "He's not sick. If he were sick, I'd know about it. I can almost feel him think. And that wound in his forehead is almost healed. Isn't it?"

"He's just fine, honey." Frank patted her hand. "But we have these bills from the hospital . . ."

Ari ignored this. "If Chase is healthy, it's okay. You can tell me anything."

Ann cleared her throat. "You know the Carmichaels."

"That rich guy and his daughter? You've told me about them."

"We — she's taken a shine to Chase."

"Anyone would," Ari said lovingly.

42

"And they've offered us a lot of money to lease him for a year."

"What?" Ari was aware that her voice was soft and her tone mild. "You said no, of course."

"We're not selling him, or anything like that, of course!" Frank said in a shocked way. "This lease is just like rent. He'll be right here at Glacier River Farm. They won't own him, or anything like that. I mean, he's not ours to sell."

"He's *mine*!" Ari burst out.

"He's not yours to sell, either, milady," Ann said gently. "But we need the cash bad, Ari."

"Lease her another horse," Ari said.

"She doesn't want another horse," Frank said. He wriggled in his chair. He was very upset, Ari could see. She could also see that no one would want another horse if Chase were around.

"Well, she can't have him," Ari said flatly. "He's special. He's *mine*!"

Frank shrugged. "He's just another horse now, Ari, without his . . ."

"Frank!" Ann said warningly. "You know Dr. Bohnes said she has to remember all by herself. Or it won't stick." She leaned over and patted Ari's hand. "I'm sorry. I'm real sorry. But we don't know what else to do. We gotta eat, Ari. And this is the only way we know how to make money. Please, honey. Please. You've got a month more. Then they take him."

The bills. The hospital bills. They were her fault. But she had a month. Four weeks when she didn't have to think about it. And, holding back hot tears, Ari said, "All right."

She thought the words would choke her.

7

The sun rose over Glacier River Farm, washing pale color over the green pastures and turning the white fences to butter-yellow. Linc walked down the gravel path to the stream that bordered the woods surrounding the barns and old gray house.

"Linc! Lincoln!" Ari's voice had wisdom and a warm authority in it. The dog turned eagerly. The call came from a thick stand of pines that stood just beyond the small waterfall that fed Glacier Brook. He cocked his head, and his ears tuliped forward.

"L-i-i-incoln!" Ari and Chase cantered out of the trees and into the sunlight. She drew in the reins, stopped, and smiled at the collie. "Where have you been?" she teased him. "Chase and I have been out for miles. And you missed it all, Linc."

The dog raised his muzzle and barked happily. Ari snapped her fingers lightly, and the dog pranced to her side.

Ari wore breeches, high black boots, and a faded T-shirt. The sun glanced off the ruby jewel suspended from a gold chain at her throat. She had left her hair unbound this morning, and it swept past her waist and just touched the back of her saddle. The great horse she rode bent his neck and danced as the collie approached. Ari swayed gracefully in the saddle and flexed the reins. "Easy now, Chase," she said. Amusement colored her tones. "You know Linc."

The horse snorted and pawed the ground, arrogance in the set of his head and neck. *Ah, yes, I know him,* he seemed to say. *But will he obey the Great Me?*

Ari settled into the saddle and quieted Chase to a full halt. She patted her left thigh. Linc rose on his hindquarters, resting his front paws against thickly padded girth. Chase shook his head irritably but stayed quiet under her hands. Ari scratched the collie's nose affectionately. "I want you both to be good today," she said softly. "I know neither of you is going to understand what will happen. But you have to bear it. You have to bear it for my sake." Linc dropped to the ground and cocked his head to one side. His forehead wrinkled with a question. "Our month is up. And we've got a problem. It's a girl who takes riding lessons here. Her name is Lori Carmichael."

Linc growled a little. Chase shifted on his hooves.

"She met Chase while I was laid up with these stupid legs of mine. She really . . . likes him." Ari took a deep breath and fought back tears. She had to act normally, for her animals' sake. "Her parents have taken out a lease on you, Chase. They're paying a lot of money so that she can ride you for a year. And the farm needs the money. This . . ." She swallowed hard, the tears she'd sworn she'd never shed now rising in her throat. She stroked the horse's neck. "This is our last ride, Chase. Just for a while, that is. This morning, Lori's coming over and I'm going to give her a lesson, to show her how to ride you." She sat a little straighter in the saddle. "So. I still own you, Chase. I've just had to lend you out a bit. Frank and Ann need the money for my medical bills, and there's no other way for me to raise it. I'm so sorry. I'm so dreadfully sorry. But there's no other way around it. Now, both of you are going to behave, aren't you? Linc? Chase?"

The collie barked. Chase flicked one ear back. Ari waited a moment for her voice to come under control. "We'll be late for morning chores," Ari said to the both of them. "Let's ride!" She touched her heels lightly to Chase's side, and they cantered toward the big barn that formed the heart of Glacier River Farm. Chase jumped the three-board fence that bordered the south pasture with careless ease, but the fence was too high for Linc. The collie grumbled softly under his breath, then wriggled through between the two lowest boards. Ari glanced over her shoulder and grinned to herself. The big dog was fastidious, and he hated to get his coat rumpled. She'd brush him after she cooled Chase out.

As horse and girl swept through the pasture, Ari kept a keen eye on the ground ahead. Here, the grass was knee-high, due to be mowed for hay. The heavy growth disguised the earth and would conceal any woodchuck holes that might trip the great chestnut stallion up. But more than that, there was something about this spot that suddenly disturbed her. She didn't know why, just that this place, a mile or more from the safety of the farm itself, was eerily quiet. No birds sang here, and the wildflowers were scarce.

She flexed Chase to a walk. She wasn't anxious to get back on this, her last free morning on her stallion.

At first, the sound was no more than a breath on the wind sailing past her ears:

Arianna, Arianna, Arianna.

She drove her back lightly into the saddle and flexed the reins to check Chase's forward stride. Yes, there it was again. Her name, sailing the breeze.

Arianna!

"Yes?" she said. She came to a full halt and turned in the saddle. The pasture was quiet under the morning sun. Unnaturally quiet for this already spooky place. Even the breeze was stilled. It was as if the world held its breath.

Chase curvetted under her hand. She sat easily erect as he turned in a circle.

Nothing stirred. Nothing at all. Then, to her astonishment, she heard a quarrel: two voices — one low, angry, and hissing, the other high and panicked. Ari's throat tightened. The grass here was high, but not high enough to conceal a person, not even a small child. Where were the voices coming from? And what was the quarrel about? She couldn't distinguish the words, just the pitch of the two speakers. She guessed the fight was over something that the high-voiced one had, which the hisser wanted badly.

Suddenly, Lincoln dashed forward, barking furiously. He leaped into a stand of taller grass that grew just in front of them. The high-pitched voice shrieked. Lincoln's deep barks turned to angry growls.

"Lincoln!" Ari swung out of the saddle, wincing a little as her bad leg hit the ground. She held Chase's reins in one hand and walked forward. Her heart was hammering in her chest, but she said calmly, "Hello? Is anyone there?"

Lincoln's barks stopped abruptly, as if a brutal hand had closed around his throat. Fear for her pet drove Ari forward. "Lincoln," she called firmly. "Here, boy."

There was no movement in the clump of grass, just a flash of Lincoln's gold-and-black coat.

And something else. A shadow slipped through the grass. Quietly. Slyly.

She took a deep breath. A terrible odor hit her like a blow. Dark, fetid, and bloody. Chase shrilled a high, warning whinny. He threw his great bronze body in front of hers and she reeled backward, landing on the ground with a painful thud.

"Whoa, Chase," she said, in an I-really-mean-it voice. "You *stand*."

The horse flung his head up and down, up and down, the odd white scar on his forehead catching the sunlight like a prism. But he obeyed her and stood trembling as she dropped the reins and walked forward to the brush that concealed her dog.

She knelt and parted the grass with both hands. Lincoln bolted out of the grass, his jaws speckled with a dark, oily liquid that gave off that hideous smell, his barks splitting the air like a hammer. Behind him, the hissing voice rose in a frustrated wail: *Give it back!*

The dog snarled, almost if he were saying, *No!*

Ari grabbed Linc's ruff with both hands. "You *sit*," she told him.

He sat, his brown eyes desperate. He raised one white forepaw and clawed urgently at her knees.

"It's okay," she soothed him. "It's *okay*." Gently, she pushed him aside and bent forward. She parted the long grass. Whatever it was lay coiled in a

50

stinking puddle just beneath her searching hand. She held back a scream and took a deep breath. She narrowed her eyes, trying to bring whatever it was into focus, but the black and oily substance shifted, twisted, and coiled like a snake. Impossible to make out the shape.

She bent lower, her hair falling around her cheeks. The blackness spun in a whirlpool that burrowed deep into the earth. And at the bottom of the pool was a red-rimmed, fiery eye. The eye turned, rolled, searched the air above her. Saw her. And fastened its hideous gaze on her face.

Fear hit Ari like a tidal wave. It engulfed her: cold, relentless, unimaginable. She struggled with the fear like a rabbit in the jaws of a snake. She forced her hands over her own eyes, to shut out that terrible searching gaze.

Then a whisper came out of the air over her shoulder, from the first speaker. An older man, perhaps? *Come back, Arianna. Come back.*

Ari straightened her shoulders and took her hands from her face. Whatever was going on, it was better to face it than to hide. She spun around. Her dog and her horse looked back at her. There was nothing else in the meadow. She forced herself to turn to the terrible pool and the red-rimmed eye in its depths. Ari swallowed the sickness rising in her throat and said, too loudly, "Get out of here. Go on. GET! Both of you!"

The eye blinked and disappeared. Nothing

51

remained of the oily pool. No scent. No sound. And the voice on the breeze was gone. Her fear receded. Just like a wave at the beach, it ebbed and flowed away.

Ari sat back on her heels, frowning. Her heartbeats slowed to normal. She got up and ran swift hands over Chase's back and legs: He was okay at least. She turned to Linc, who waited patiently as she explored his fur with quick fingers. No cuts. No bruises. If that *thing* had been trapped somehow, it hadn't hurt the dog. Then she felt something deep in the fur at Linc's throat. She tugged it carefully free and turned it over in her palm.

"What's this?!" she said. "Look at this!" She held it up so that the sun struck white light from it. A twisted shell of silver, the size of charms on a necklace. The charm was about an inch and a half long and no more than an eighth of an inch wide. It was the long, pointy sort of shell that might have held a very thin snail. Ari held it up and admired it.

Chase whinnied. Ari jumped a little at the sound. Chase whinnied again, more urgently. Ari looked at her watch. "Uh-oh. You're right, Chase. We *are* going to be late!" She tucked the tiny shell in her shirt pocket and scrambled to her feet. If she was very late, poor Ann would be as mad as fire. Ari knew how hard it was, making a living on a horse farm, even one as beautiful and big as Glacier River.

Ari remounted, and the three of them headed home.

8

Just a few minutes later, Ari and Chase leaped the five-bar gate in the fence that bordered the farmyard. Ann came out of the barn at the sound of hooves on the driveway.

"You were gone awhile," she said. Ari noticed that Ann had patched her jeans with duct tape. No wonder Ann and Frank hadn't been able to resist the huge amount of money Lori's parents were willing to pay the farm to lease Chase for Lori's private use.

Ari closed her eyes briefly against the familiar stab of pain: Chase being leased, *used*, by a stranger. She shoved the thoughts out of her head and smiled down at Ann.

"Thought you might have fallen off." Ann's eyes were bright and curious.

"Off Chase?" Ari kept her voice warm. "Never." She hesitated. Should she tell Ann about the strange incident in the pasture?

Ann shot a swift, secretive glance toward Ari's legs in their breeches and high black boots. "A person never knows what you're up to," she said. Her mouth thinned in affectionate annoyance. "And I worry about you." Then Ann asked, "How are your legs? The hospital called about getting a new set of X rays."

Oh, my, Ari thought. X rays were expensive. It's a bad day for her already. She doesn't need to hear about that creepy eye. "My legs feel fine this morning," Ari lied. "I don't need any more X rays." She swung out of the saddle and dropped to the ground. It was an effort, but she kept the pain out of her face. "A few more weeks of riding, and you'll never know that I've been in an accident."

That strange, flickering glance at her legs again. Ann ducked her head. Ari knew Ann didn't believe her. "Well," she said with a brave smile, "I'm sure we all hope so. But you must be careful, my . . ." She stopped herself. "Ari," she added.

Ari wished for the thousandth time that she could remember her life before the accident that broke her legs and gave her a concussion. That she could recall her mother and her father. That she knew why, out of all the foster parents that the county social services department could have chosen, she'd been placed here with Ann and Frank, who never seemed to know how to deal with her. Who had treated her with a weird mixture of love and respect in the three slow, painful months of recovery she had spent here already.

"I think the orthopedist will be pleased when he sees me next week, Ann. We managed to jump five fences this morning, Chase and I. And we galloped for a good twenty minutes."

"Cool him out really well before the Carmichaels get here," Ann suggested. Then she said with mock bossiness, "And you get to cleaning those stalls quick, you hear?"

"You bet," Ari said cheerfully. She looped Chase's reins into one hand and walked him into the barn.

She took Chase down the aisle to the wash racks, past the stalls lining either side. She didn't remember anything about her life before the accident, but she knew she must have loved this place. Each stall was made of varnished oak, with black iron hayracks and black barred doors. Most of the horses were turned out to pasture. They'd been in their stalls all night. Ari had volunteered to clean out the manure and put fresh bedding in for them before they came in from pasture. Their names were on brass plates over the doors: MAX, SCOOTER, SHY-NO-MORE, BEECHER, and CINNAMON — the names went on and on.

She led Chase to the cool-water wash rack and took off his saddle and bridle. She hooked him into the cross ties and turned the shower on. Lincoln curled into the corner with a heavy sigh. Ari suppressed a giggle. Lincoln was resigned to what the rest of the morning would bring: the routine that went on day after day, cooling down, mucking out, training the young horses on the longe line. It'd be hours before she'd have time to brush Linc and clean his white forepaws. And Lori Carmichael would be coming this morning for her first lesson on Chase.

Ari frowned at that and stroked the great horse's neck. She was going to do her best to talk Lori out of using a harsh bit on Chase. Frank had admitted Lori wasn't a very good rider. Lori would want to use the harshest bit she could, since that was an easy way for a bad rider to get control of a horse that knew more than the rider did.

Chase turned and looked at her, a question in his deep brown eyes.

"It'll be a short lesson, Chase. I promise." He was a huge horse, close to seventeen hands high, and she had to stand on tiptoe to whisper in his ear. She ignored the spray of water down her back. "And I'll make sure she uses a snaffle today. You know that if it were up to me, I'd throw all the Carmichaels off the farm, don't you?"

He nodded, as if he understood. Ari ran her hands down his satiny neck, then over the white scar in the center of his forehead. That was the thing about Chase. He always understood.

In the months she'd spent recovering, Ari

had relearned Glacier River Farm and how it worked. Ann and Frank boarded and trained more than forty horses at the farm. Frank said that the farm had everything a horse owner could want, and more. The pastures were green and smooth, with triple-barred white fences all around. The buildings — barns, house, and indoor arena — were built of a warm red brick that glowed in the sun and was softened by rain. The farm veterinarian, Dr. Bohnes, had her own special office with a little clinic for injured horses in the boarder barn. There was even a small restaurant that was open for lunch and dinner for horse shows.

And, of course, there were trails. Miles and miles of trails. Ari and Dr. Bohnes had explored the strange, twisting roads that wound through the woods and valleys of the farm one afternoon. Dr. Bohnes had pushed Ari in a wheelchair. Some of the trails seemed to lead nowhere. At other times they seemed to lead everywhere. Ari had asked Dr. Bohnes about the unexpected caves and tunnels that filled the woods. She told the vet how they pulled at her — especially the cave in the south pasture.

Remembering now, she paused, one hand on Chase's neck. The south pasture. Where she'd seen that awful eye.

The old vet hadn't seemed surprised. But she'd warned Ari away from the tunnels. Millions of years ago, the glaciers moved through the land here like titanic ghost ships. As they moved, the land swelled under the glaciers like ocean waves, rising, falling, and folding itself to help smooth the glaciers' path to the sea beyond. The huge icebergs had long gone, but they'd left caves and tunnels under the softly swelling hills.

Ari was drawn to them in a way she couldn't explain. She'd told Frank about her need to explore, to find her way through them, and he'd given her an alarmed look. He was a mild-mannered man, and anxious. Worry lines creased his forehead, drew deep grooves on either side of his mouth. They got even more prominent when she'd told him about the way the caves seem to draw her in, beckoning.

"You can't!" he'd said, leaning forward, so close she could feel his breath. "You *stay away from them*!"

"Lincoln wouldn't let me get lost," she'd replied, frowning at the strangeness of his reaction. "He'd lead me home. And so would Chase."

Except that Chase wasn't hers anymore. You've got to remember that, she told herself.

"I remember that," Ari said aloud, softly. "I may not remember anything else, but I remember that." She wiped the water away from Chase's neck. His mane was long and gleaming. "How could I forget you belong to someone else now?" She touched the silver shell in her pocket. It lay there, warm under her hand. "Oh, Chase," she said sadly. "How can I remember if I belong anywhere? Or to anyone?"

She rolled the shell in her hand. It felt warm, almost hot.

"There's something," she murmured aloud. "There's something I'm supposed to do! Somewhere I'm supposed to go! Chase. Help me!"

The big horse rested his muzzle on her shoulder and breathed softly into her hair. But he didn't have an answer.

9

"Just take it easy, Princess," Mr. Carmichael shouted across the arena. "And if the horse gives you any trouble, give him the whip."

Lori Carmichael scowled and said, "For goodness *sake*, Dad," and bent to brush her spotless riding boots with a towel. She was shorter than Ari, and sturdily built. Her hair was white-blond and drawn back in a tight bun low on her neck. "Aren't you ready yet?" she snapped at Ari.

Ari hated her on sight.

The three of them, Chase, Ari, and Lori, were in the middle of the huge indoor arena, the center of all the riding activities at Glacier River Farm. Six inches of sand covered the floor. This made a cushioned footing for the horses. The building itself was huge. The rafters soared thirty feet high at the peak. They dropped to twenty feet at the walls to meet the bleachers that surrounded the arena on three sides. Mr. Carmichael, his wife, and Lori's older brother sat in the judge's box, where celebrities gathered at official horse shows when the prizes were given out.

"Let's *go*," Lori demanded. "Give me a leg up, will you?"

"You'll remember not to pull at his mouth," Ari said quietly. "And keep your weight off his back unless you want him to turn or stop."

"Excuse me?" Lori said. She lifted one eyebrow. Her eyes narrowed in sarcasm. "My father turned the check over to Frank five minutes ago. Which means this horse is *mine*."

Ari couldn't stop herself. All her good resolutions about accepting the lease agreement with courage went flying. "It's just for a year," she said. "And the agreement was that he's yours only when you come to the farm." She was angry, but she kept her gestures calm and her expression unexcited. "Could you wait a second, please? I'll just check the length of the stirrup leathers." Ari gave Lori a polite smile and moved closer to Chase. She slid one hand over his sleek withers and murmured so that only the horse could hear. "Please, Chase. Listen to me when she gets on. Listen to *me*."

She stepped back, handed the reins to Lori, and cupped her hands together to give Lori a leg up. The girl planted one black-booted foot in Ari's palm and heaved herself onto Chase's back. A short whip dangled from one wrist. She dropped into the saddle with a thump. She clutched the reins and pulled. Chase tossed his head and backed up.

"Whoa, now," Ari said. "Walk on, Chase."

The bronze horse shook his head from side to side, the harsh bit Lori's father had insisted on jingling in his mouth. Lori gave a small shriek and clapped both heels against his sides. Chase raised his muzzle and rolled his eye back so that the whites showed.

"Just sit still," Ari said, more loudly than she'd meant to. "He's never had anyone on his back but me. And he's not used to . . ."

"He'll just have to *get* used to it," Lori snarled. She sawed the reins back and forth, back and forth, a technique good riders use in only the most extreme circumstances. Ari had never used it on Chase. Even with the mild snaffle bit in his mouth, it would have hurt to have cold iron drawn harshly over his teeth. This cruel copper bit was much, much worse. If Lori kept it up, his mouth would bleed.

"Easy," Ari said. "Please, Chase."

Sweat patched the great animal's shoulders. He shuddered, his ears turned to Ari's voice. He danced on the tips of his hooves.

"What's *wrong* with him?" Lori yelled. "You've done something to him!" She jounced uncomfortably, her legs banging against Chase's side. Ari saw she was beginning to panic. In the stands, Linc began to bark.

"You keep that blasted animal under control," Mr. Carmichael shouted. "Give him the whip, Princess. Give him the whip!"

Chase whinnied, a low, urgent, what's-happening-here sort of noise.

Ari bit her lip and walked toward them, hand outstretched. "Why don't you slide off, and we'll try again tomorrow, Lori?" she suggested. "It might be a good idea if you helped groom him and saddle him, for instance. It'll give him a chance to get to know you bet —" She stopped in midsentence. Chase gathered himself together. His muscled haunches bulged. His chest expanded with the effort of keeping his forelegs safely on the ground. Ari knew what those signs meant. "Easy. Please, Chase. Listen to me."

Lori raised her right arm, the crop in her hand. Ari stiffened and shouted out, "NO!"

The whip descended onto Chase's back.

Chase went berserk. He put his nose to the ground. His hind legs flew out and up. Lori slid forward over his neck, screaming. He reared back, forelegs reaching to the roof. Lori slid back in the saddle, both hands clutching his mane, her feet dangling free from the stirrups. Ari heard the *thump* of running feet from the stands, Linc's deep barks, and Mr. Carmichael shouting, "Lori. *Lori*. LORI!"

Lori sawed frantically at the reins. Chase's jaws were wide open, blood-flecked foam spraying over his neck, spotting the strange white scar on his forehead. He pitched up and down, eyes furious, the breath exploding from his nostrils. His ears lay flat against his skull.

Ari moved fast. She came to a stop directly in front of the giant horse. She raised both hands, ignoring the pain in her legs, her voice level. "Whoa, boy. You *stand*!"

Chase's ears flicked forward.

"You hear me, don't you?" Ari commanded. "Stand, please!"

Chase stood. He dropped his head, sighing. A little blood trickled over his muzzle.

Lori slumped over his neck, crying in a loud way. Ari stepped up to Chase, looped the reins in one hand, and stroked his chest with the other. She could feel him trembling. She soothed him gently as Frank and Mr. Carmichael ran across the arena and up to them.

"Outta the way, girl!" Mr. Carmichael shoved Ari aside and grabbed Lori. "Lori! Lori, baby! Are you all right?" He pulled his daughter from the saddle and set her on the ground. Then he hugged her, his back to Ari. Lori glared at Ari over her father's shoulder.

"Well!" Frank said. One thin hand tugged nervously at his long brown mustache. The other twisted the top button of his denim shirt. "Doesn't seem as though anyone was hurt. Does it?"

Mr. Carmichael whirled, holding Lori tight to his side. "How dare you put my daughter on that horse! It's unsafe! He could have killed her!" His fat face grew dark with rage. "I want him shot!"

Ari clutched the reins. Chase's head went up. His ears went forward. He stared straight at Mr. Carmichael.

And a voice bellowed angrily in Ari's mind: *Little man!*

She looked at Chase, hardly believing what the voice in her head must mean.

The horse pawed at the arena floor. Again, Ari heard his voice inside her head:

You shall be dirt beneath my hooves, little man.

"Chase?" she wondered aloud. "Chase?!"

He turned to her, his gaze direct and angry. His nostrils flared red. He reared, pulling the reins from Ari's hands. Then he dropped his head low to the ground and swung his head from side to side, the way a stallion will when he is ready to strike at an enemy. He pawed at the ground with his iron hooves. *I will crush his bones with the Snake!*

"But they'll shoot you!" she said. And then to herself, *I can't believe this. I won't believe this. Is Chase talking to me?* She put her hands over her eyes, to quiet her thoughts. She dropped them abruptly when Mr. Carmichael stormed, "I'm getting the gun. Where's the gun, Frank? I want the darn *gun.*"

Lori shrieked, "Shoot him, Daddy. Shoot him!"

"No one is going to shoot anyone here," Ari said with quiet authority. "Chase. You stand, please. Please, boy. For my sake!"

For a long, agonizing moment, she didn't think the command would work. Then the great stallion took a shuddering breath and stood still.

Ari kept her eyes on his every move. Moving slowly, she picked up the reins and walked toward him. "Are you all right now?"

Chase looked down, his eyes calm, his flanks moving in and out with regular, easy breaths.

"Chase?"

No answer in her mind. Perhaps she had been dreaming. Ari shook her head briefly to clear it. She'd been nuts to think that he had spoken to her. She ran her hand down Chase's neck, then turned to walk him back to his stall.

"Just a minute there, young lady." Mr. Carmichael folded his arms across his chest and glared at her. Lori leaned against him, her cheek pushed into the shoulder of his sport coat. She gave Ari a measuring kind of look.

"Oh. Of course. The check. You'll want that back." Ari fumbled in her jeans pocket, then remembered Mr. Carmichael had given the check to Frank. She looked at him. "I'm sorry the lease didn't work out."

Lori pushed herself away from her father and whined, "But I want to ride Chase, Daddy. And I *can* ride him. That horse isn't going to listen to me with her around." She jerked her chin at Ari. "She made Chase throw me off."

"He didn't throw you off," Ari said. "You fell off. There's a big difference."

"She did it on purpose, Daddy. I know she did. She wouldn't let me ride him with the right kind of bit. He can't stand that copper bit. Look how his mouth is bleeding."

"*You* made me put that bit in his mouth!" Ari said, astonished. "Why are you lying?"

"I'm not lying. You're the one who's lying. You're the one that trained that horse to make me look like a jerk. It's because you don't want me to have him! You want to have him all to yourself."

"That's not true," Ari said.

"Now, Ari. Now, Ari." Frank put his hand on her shoulder. "I know you're unhappy with this leasing agreement, but we've talked about it. Remember? With your legs so busted up right now, it isn't really possible for you to ride the horse as much as he needs to be ridden to keep fit. If you look at it one way, the Carmichaels are doing us a big favor."

Ari stared at him. She knew Frank was embarrassed by needing the money from the lease to keep Glacier River Farm up and running. But to blame Lori's bad riding on her!

"Here." Mr. Carmichael shoved Frank with one finger. "We'll keep the horse. But my little girl here is right. The horse hasn't been trained properly. Give him here." He snatched the reins from Ari's hand before she could move. "We'll call around, Princess. And we'll find a real trainer to knock some sense into this animal." He jerked hard on the reins. "Come on, you."

Chase dug both front hooves into the sand and pulled his head back. He wasn't upset, Ari saw, just wondering what the heck was going on.

"Make him come with you, Daddy," Lori whined. "Wait! I'll get back on. You hold him!" She remounted, smiling angelically at her father.

"Move, darn you!" Mr. Carmichael jerked again. Chase didn't budge. He stood looking down at all of them, splendid head held high. Mr. Carmichael took the lower part of the reins in one hand then swung them around. The loose reins came down hard. The blow raised a thin welt on Chase's glossy neck and he jumped back, snorting. He was still puzzled, Ari saw.

And she knew why he was confused.

Ari didn't remember anything about her life before the accident that crippled her legs. Not her mother; not her father. Not even if she had any brothers or sisters. But she did know that she had always owned Chase. He was as much a part of her as her heart, or her lungs, or her hands. And she knew that she had never, ever laid a hand or a whip on him. Which was why he was calm now. He didn't believe anyone would hurt him deliberately. She could almost hear his thoughts — not in the way she had heard his voice a few moments ago, but because she loved him. And that love let her understand him the way she could understand no one else. His expression told her: *The pain from the slashing reins was an accident. Wasn't it?*

Mr. Carmichael jerked on the reins to make Chase come forward. Obediently, the big horse stepped closer. With the horse directly in front of him now, Mr. Carmichael swung the reins and struck. Blood welled against Chase's golden neck in a thin trickle. It was only a matter of seconds before he lost his temper. Mr. Carmichael was a fool to think he could control an angry fourteen-hundred-pound stallion with anything but a gun. What might happen after Chase exploded was unthinkable. Lori, her face pale, jumped off.

Ari thought fast. There was only one thing she could do.

Suddenly, Ari shouted, "Linc!" Lincoln bounded down from the bleachers in three giant leaps and flew toward her, a gold-and-black blur. She pointed at Mr. Carmichael. Linc laid his ears back and growled. Mr. Carmichael dropped the reins with a yelp. Ari sprang forward, scooped up Chase's reins, and leaped into the saddle. She urged Chase into a hand gallop. With Lincoln streaking beside them, Ari guided the horse to the south end of the arena, which was open to the soft summer air.

Ari galloped to the clinic. Then she pulled Chase up and sat quietly. Lincoln settled gravely on the gravel drive, forepaws extended. He cocked his head and looked at her. She sighed and ran one hand through her long hair. "I hated to do that, Chase."

Chase shifted underneath her. Lincoln lifted his head to look at her.

"I know. I know. It's a terrible thing I did. Ann and Frank are going to be really upset. But what else could I do? You saw how Mr. Carmichael was beating Chase."

Lincoln rumbled — a cross between a growl and a low bark. He curled his upper lip a little so that she could see the point of one ivory-colored eyetooth.

Ari added hopefully, "Maybe Lori and her father will be so upset they'll forget all about the lease."

The collie sneezed. It was more of a snort than a sneeze, the kind of snort that meant *yeah, right!* in a very sarcastic way. Ari slipped out of the saddle and knelt beside her dog. She ran her hands lovingly through his creamy ruff. "Are you talking to me, too, now?" She laughed a little sadly. "I don't know, guys. The both of you talking to me? Phooey. Maybe I'm just going flat-out crazy." She bent and kissed the tawny spot right in the middle of Linc's forehead. Chase nudged her shoulder with his nose. Behind her, she could hear loud, angry voices: Mr. Carmichael shouting at Frank, Lori shouting at her father.

Ari stood up a little straighter and looped

Chase's reins over her arm. She'd have to take Chase back into the arena and face them all. But not now. The scars on her legs throbbed with a fierce pain. She closed her eyes and bit her lip to keep from crying out.

Everything was going totally wrong.

10

"Just stand there a bit," a fussy voice said at her elbow. "I've told you before. Those are just muscle spasms. It hurts now, but it shows your legs are healing."

Ari opened her eyes and smiled. Dr. Bohnes had come out of the clinic, attracted by the noise and the shouting. "Hi, Dr. Bohnes."

The little vet jigged back and forth from one foot to the other. Ari would never say it aloud, but the way Dr. Bohnes dressed made her want to laugh. She liked bright-colored shirts, leather sandals, and long, baggy skirts. Her hair was pure, brilliant white, cut short. It curled over her pink skull like a wispy cloud. Ari hadn't seen Dr. Bohnes yet today, what with one thing and another. This morning's shirt was a bright, tie-dyed orange, yellow, and red. Ari didn't know how old she was. But she would be Ari's grandmother's age, at least. Ari blinked back tears.

She couldn't even remember if she had a grand-mother.

"Older than that, milady," Dr. Bohnes said cheerfully.

"That makes three of you today," Ari said with surprise. She smiled. She didn't mind Dr. Bohnes calling her milady. She always did. And it made her feel less alone somehow.

"Three of us what?" Dr. Bohnes demanded.

"Reading my thoughts."

"Oh?" Her bright blue eyes sharpened. She looked at Lincoln and then at Chase. "And what kind of thoughts were you having, that the animals could read them?"

"Never mind." Ari nodded toward the arena. Ann had joined the quarrel, and the voices were even louder. "There's been kind of an upset this morning. Maybe I just imagined it."

"Hah! I told Frank and Ann not to lease Chase out. Especially to those dratted Carmichaels." She snorted, with far more gruffness than Lincoln had. "That horse never tolerated anyone on his back but you. And he never will."

"I thought he would if I asked him," Ari said simply. "And we need the money, Dr. Bohnes."

"We wouldn't if —" She bit off what she was going to say.

"If what?"

"Never mind. Come along. It's past time to massage your legs."

73

"But . . ." Ari looked toward the arena building. The argument had drifted outside. Mr. Carmichael and Lori were gathered around Frank. Mr. Carmichael was waving his arms and yelling about how dangerous Chase was. "I should . . ."

"Nothing you can do there," Dr. Bohnes said briskly. "And if you ask me, it's better to get Chase out of sight."

This made sense. Dr. Bohnes almost always made sense. Ari took Chase and followed her colorful, tiny figure past the round pen and to the back of the big barn, where the elderly vet kept her little clinic.

Although Dr. Bohnes was a horse vet, injured or sick animals from miles around eventually found their way to the bright blue door of her clinic. There was a short line there today: the little boy from the Peterson farm up the road with a fat calico cat; a sorry-looking yellow dog with a sore paw; a motherly lady with a parakeet perched on her shoulder. The parakeet squawked angrily at the cat, who opened its golden eyes once, snarled, then went back to sleep in its owner's arms.

"Huh!" Dr. Bohnes grumbled. This meant she was irritated at all the work in front of her. "Sponge Chase down, Ari, and put some of that sticky salve on the cuts in his mouth. You know, it's the same stuff I use on your legs. Then turn him out, won't you? By the time you've finished with that, I'll get through this lot here."

74

Ari gave her a quick hug, smiled at the little Peterson boy, and took Chase to the small paddock where Dr. Bohnes treated the larger animals. She removed his bridle and haltered him, then asked him to stand while she fetched warm water and the sticky salve. Ari didn't know of any other horse that would obey the "stand" command as well as Chase did. She'd never known him once to break it.

Lincoln followed Ari into the storeroom, where the vet kept her medicines. Ari loved the scents of the storeroom. Dr. Bohnes mixed many of her own salves and poultices from herbs, nuts, and berries that she grew in a special garden. The air was filled with the sharp scent of arrowroot, a lingering odor of lavender, and something roselike.

Ari inhaled with delight. Linc took a breath and sneezed. Ari grinned to herself and searched the shelves for the midnight-colored cream that Dr. Bohnes used to heal her scars from the accident. Her hands were quick, sorting through the jars and herb bags on the shelves. She picked up a small ceramic pot so that she could reach for the large canister of salve against the back wall.

A horrible smell hit her like a fist. Her hand loosened and the pot fell. Ari made a hasty grab to catch it before it smashed onto the flagstone floor. Behind her, the dog growled, then barked. Ari caught the jar just in time and looked at it, puzzled. She'd never seen anything like it on the vet's shelves before. The closer she looked at it, the harder it was

75

to see just what color the pot was: flame-red? Sickly yellow-green? And was that where the terrible stink came from? Curious, Ari tugged at the cork stopper.

Lincoln leaped to her side and pushed his nose against her wrist. His snarls twisted like snakes, if snakes had been sounds.

"Just a minute, Linc," she said. "Easy, now." She hesitated. She was pretty sure that the vet had nothing truly dangerous out in the open. But maybe she'd had this curious thing locked up somewhere and forgotten to put it back.

The urge to open the pot was powerful. Something, *something* twisted her fingers around the top, as if . . . as if a huge, clawed hand — invisible, powerful, mean — were forcing her to open it.

Ari pulled off the stopper and looked in.

At first, she saw nothing but dark. Then a thin coil of acid smoke rose from the depths of the jar. There were shapes in the smoke. Ari was sure of it. She held the jar up and watched the shapes spiral toward the low ceiling. Lincoln barked and barked. The smoke curled around her face, slid past her nose, poured into her eyes.

And she saw . . . she heard . . .

She was in the center of nighttime, in a place she'd never been before. The sky was dark and starless. At her feet was a humped mound, blacker than the black night sky. The mound shifted, moved, then screamed with the sound of a million hornets. Ari jumped and shouted with surprise. The mound at her feet swelled, grew, unfolded like an evil flower. And an eye formed in the center of the hooded blackness, a green-and-yellow eye, multifaceted, like some grotesque and terrible insect. The same terrible vision she'd seen in the meadow!

Where are you? a thousand voices whispered. The eye rolled in its bloodied socket, searching, searching. . . .

It was all Ari could do to hold onto the pot. She was dimly aware of Linc's excited barking, the dashes he was making to get out of the range of that terrible eye. The rest of her world faded, leaving her to this terrifying encounter. She took a deep breath, then another . . .

And fainted.

11

"Tell me what you saw," Dr. Bohnes demanded. "Everything." She peered into Ari's face. Ari was lying on the old leather couch in the vet's office.

"Chase?" she said aloud. Her voice was foggy. She cleared her throat.

"He's fine," Dr. Bohnes said impatiently. Her strong old hand closed around Ari's wrist. Her grip was warm.

Ari focused on the fierce blue eyes. "What happened? It wasn't —" She forced the words out. "I haven't been in another accident?"

Were there tears in those wise eyes? Dr. Bohnes blinked hard. "Nonsense," she said briskly. "You're as fit as a fiddle." She pointed at the collie, sitting anxiously next to the couch. "Lincoln here was barking fit to raise the . . . that is, fit to bust. When I came into the storeroom, I found you on the floor."

78

"The pot," Ari said.

"What about the pot?"

"Did it break? There was something awful in it, and something terrible was after me. . . ." Ari trailed off. She tried to concentrate. She remembered the eye. The yellow-green eye that was searching, searching. The feeling that if it saw her, it would pierce her to the heart. And the buzzing of angry hornets. She shivered. "I opened the ceramic pot. The one with the funny smell. It was an awful smell, to tell you the truth. I can't imagine what that kind of medicine would be for."

"There was no ceramic pot." The vet's voice was firm. "Nothing like that at all on my shelves. Ari, *you must tell me* what you saw."

Ari ran her hands through her hair. The back of her neck was sweaty. "Insects," she said in a small voice. "Hornets, or maybe wasps. It was dark. Really dark. And this horrible yellow-green . . ."

"Yellow-green what?" Dr. Bohnes commanded.

Ari opened her mouth to tell her. She couldn't get the words out. It was as if they were stuck in molasses. She knew — somehow she knew — that if she could tell Dr. Bohnes about the hideous eye, she would be safe, safe from it, because . . .

"It . . ." she struggled. "It was . . . looking . . ." Her brain felt as if it were wading through hip-deep mud. Suddenly, she broke free of the strange lock on her tongue and gasped, "Look . . . looking FOR ME!"

Dr. Bohnes turned pale and started to speak.

"Ari!" Ann opened the clinic door with a bang and thudded into the room. She wore green rubber boots plastered with manure. Her hair was sticking to her skull with sweat. "There you are! It's past time for four o'clock chores, so I started without you. Have you been here all this time?"

Ari struggled to sit up. The whole afternoon gone? Fear clutched her heart. In the days after the accident, there had been many days like that, when she had drifted in and out of consciousness, not knowing where the time had gone. She buried one hand in Lincoln's soft fur. He whined and licked her wrist with his warm pink tongue. She couldn't, wouldn't tell either Ann or Dr. Bohnes that she'd lost all that time. She couldn't face going back to more doctors. They would question her, probe her, ask her things she couldn't answer. "I'm sorry," she said, a little surprised to find her voice so normal. "I guess I got wrapped up in taking care of Chase."

The thought of her great stallion alone in the paddock drove her to get off the couch. She sighed with relief; she was steady on her feet. She wasn't dizzy. And the dark thoughts of the eye drifted away from her like a leaf on Glacier River Brook.

"He's okay, isn't he?" Ann was anxious, Ari

could tell. "His, um, mouth is okay?" Her glance shifted nervously away from Ari's.

"Yes," Ari said. "Lori's not all that strong, thank goodness. He has two scrapes on each corner of his mouth, but they should heal."

"That's all right, then." Ann twisted her hands together. "She'll do better next time, I'm sure. With the . . . ah . . . new trainer, I mean."

Ari stared at Ann, astonished. "What?"

"Now, it's not that you aren't a wonderful trainer, but Mr. Carmichael's right. You're only thirteen, and you and the . . . um . . . horse have spent just too much time together. Far too much time. He said it isn't natural . . ." She paused, a peculiar look on her face. ". . . Not natural for that kind of bond to exist between horse and rider. And you know, he may be right. So, it will be good for both of you to have Chase handled by someone else for a change. Just for the year's lease."

Ari swallowed hard. Lincoln pressed against her knees, growling softly.

"You do understand, Ari. Don't you?"

Ari kept her eyes steadily on Ann's face. She controlled her rage with a terrific effort of will. She could feel the red in her cheeks, and her heart pound. After a long moment she said, "Do we really need the money that badly, Ann?"

Ann's eyes shifted. A long look passed between her and Dr. Bohnes. The vet said, "Pah!"

and stamped angrily to her desk. She sat down, slammed open a drawer, took out some papers, and pretended to read. Then she shouted, "I am NOT taking part in this discussion!"

Ari tried again. "Maybe I could work on the Peterson Farm, after school starts. I could earn money there. They need a stable hand."

"You have your duties here."

"I can do two jobs," Ari said stubbornly.

Neither woman looked at her legs, but Ari knew what they were thinking. She pressed on, "The healing's coming along really well, isn't it, Dr. Bohnes?"

"It is," the vet said shortly. She peered at Ann over the rim of her spectacles.

"I don't think it's a good idea for you to go off the farm just yet, Ari." Ann rubbed her neck. Her hand was muddy; it left a streak of mud between the folds of fat. "And as for school —"

"Of course I'll go to school," Ari said, astonished. "Why ever wouldn't I?"

Ann gestured vaguely. "The farm . . . the work. We were thinking of Dr. Bohnes home-schooling you."

Lincoln's growls deepened. "You make it sound as if I'm a prisoner here," she said quietly. "I haven't been off the farm since the accident except to go to the hospital. Not to the mall, not to the movies. Nowhere."

"Don't be silly!" Ann said. She chewed her lip

82

nervously. "Of course you can leave the farm. Not just now, of course. But soon."

"It's for your own safety," Dr. Bohnes said at the same time.

Ari looked from one to the other. Something was going on here. Something weird, and a little scary. "I'm going to check on Chase," she said. "And then I'll be in for dinner. Sorry I missed afternoon chores, Ann. I'll make it up to you tomorrow."

"That'll be fine," Ann mumbled. "I didn't mind. I didn't mind doing them at all."

Outside the clinic, Chase was standing with his muzzle to the air, ears up, his deep chocolate eyes gazing far into the distance. The sun was setting over Glacier River Farm. Streaks of red, pink, and gold flowed from the setting sun like water from a fountain. The green of the fields was shadowed almost to black. A few stars poked white light through the oncoming night. The white scar on Chase's forehead glowed briefly, like a firefly, and then dimmed as the sun sank in the pink ocean of light. Something . . . an animal perhaps, scrabbled briefly in the bushes planted against the grain shed at the rear of the paddock.

Ari held her breath and listened hard. She heard the slight scrape of something — feet? — on gravel. Then silence.

"Rabbit?" Ari said to Linc.

He brought his head up at that, ears tuliped forward. He grinned and wagged his tail.

"No rabbits, huh?" Ari asked.

Linc dropped his head with a disappointed sigh. Ari chuckled and let herself into the paddock. She stood beside Chase, one hand on his mighty side. Lincoln panted softly as he stood next to them. For a minute, she stood there and thought of absolutely nothing

"It's been a strange day, Chase," she said.

He whinnied.

"You seem to agree." She paused, then sent him an urgent thought with all the force of her mind. *Do you remember today? How you spoke to me in the arena?*

Chase shook himself, then dropped his muzzle to the earth and began to graze. Ari gazed at him a long moment. He seemed larger than usual, as he stood in the half dark. The twilight shadowed his haunches, traced the muscles in his broad chest. He fed quietly.

So she'd dreamed it, imagined it, maybe even had a delusion. Maybe Ann was right, and it wasn't safe for her to go away from the farm. No, that was stupid. Stupid. She wouldn't let them — any of them — talk her into questioning her own mind. She was as sane as she'd ever been. She knew it. She was as sure of that as she was of her love for her horse and her dog.

"Would you like to stay here for the night, Chase?" she asked aloud. There was a tank of clean water in the corner of the paddock, and she could bring him his hay and grain. It was pleasant here, in the evening air. And, if she had to do what she *thought* she had to do, it would be easier with him here, instead of in the big barn.

She took two flakes of hay from the stack Dr. Bohnes kept for the clinic animals and scattered them on the ground. It was good hay, timothy and clover, with a little alfalfa mixed in for flavor. Chase examined the hay with a pleased air. Ari knew he was happy because his lower lip softened, and the wrinkles above his eyes deepened. He snorted happily and stuck his nose in the pile, searching for the purple-green alfalfa blossoms before the others. Alfalfa to horses was like chocolate to people; a little was delicious, but too much meant a stomachache.

"Now, how did I know that, Linc?" she said to the collie. Perhaps her memory was coming back, in bits and pieces. Her heart lightened, and she hummed to herself as she went in search of grain for Chase's dinner.

Dr. Bohnes kept the grain locked in the shed at the back of the paddock. Ari remembered something else that she must have known before her accident: Too much grain could colic a horse. And colic could be a killer. She was careful to measure three scoops of oats and a half scoop of corn into the feed bucket. She liked the warm, cereal smell of the grain, and she ran both hands through the kernels, partly to mix the corn and oats together and partly because she liked the feel of it between her palms.

Except that grain was soft and giving. What she'd found in the middle of the oats was not. Curious, Ari stepped under the light over the back door.

Another spiraled stone. This one was creamy violet, much thicker and heavier. It was twice as long and wide as Ari's thumb. She patted her shirt pocket. Yes, there was the other stone. She took it out and laid the two together in her hand. They appeared to be made of the same stuff, but the colors of each stone were totally different: one rose, one violet. A wisp of a melody came to her and without thinking, she sang:

> *"Yellow, silver, blue*
> *The rainbow we make . . .*

— and something-something something," she muttered. Darn! She'd almost had it. The song chimed softly in the back of her mind, like a car radio set too low. She shook her head impatiently. Don't push it, Dr. Bohnes had said. Memory's like a spiderweb; push too hard and it will break. Breathe softly, and the web will hold.

A wind rose and died again, chilling the back of her neck. Suddenly, she desperately wanted the warmth and light in the farmhouse. She didn't want her memory to come back if it brought her horrible-looking eyes and strange spiraled stones and bits of songs that she couldn't complete.

She ran her hands through Chase's grain again, to make sure that no more mysterious stones lay in the bucket, and set it down for him. He looked up from the hay and hurried to the bucket, plunging his nose into the bottom. She watched him for a long moment, wrapping her arms around her body to shake off that sudden chill. She whistled to Linc, then climbed over the paddock fence and set off at a jog across the graveled drive to the house. The lights were on, and she could see Ann through the kitchen window, moving between the stove and the table. She slid her boots off by the back door, checked Linc's coat and paws for burrs, and let herself in. Frank sat in the rocking chair by the fireplace. He held a large red book in his lap, and he was frowning. Ari knew that this was the account book for the farm. It recorded all the money that Glacier River Farm took in and paid out. It was a bad sign when Frank scowled.

Ari smiled at Ann and washed her hands at the tap. "Shall I set the table?" Ann nodded abruptly. Ari had no idea why it embarrassed Ann to have her set the table, but it did. The dinner table sat in the center of the kitchen. It was made of a shiny wood that was chipped in places to reveal spongy orange wood beneath. Ari set out the cornflower blue tablecloth and the plates with the blue ladies on the rims.

She liked these plates. The center was white, but the figures circling the center were blue. Each lady was different, some slim and lovely, with long dresses and windblown hair, some curvy and smiling, with violets, roses, and silver wands in their hands. Each woman danced beneath a delicately carved arch. Above the arch was a soft drift of clouds. . . .

Ari stopped and stared at the plates, the knives, forks, and spoons for the table clutched in one hand. Crystal arch. Violet, rose, and . . . it was the song.

Had she made the song up?

She frowned. She'd seen these plates every day of her life. At least, every day of her life that she could remember. Which was the last three months. So she could imagine that she had made up a song to go with the images she'd seen.

But the melody?

The melody was like nothing she'd ever heard before.

"Ari?"

She was dimly aware that Ann was speaking to her. Lincoln nudged her urgently with his nose.

"Ari!"

She focused on Ann with a start of surprise. "Yes, Ann. Sorry. I was daydreaming, I guess."

"Are you sure you're all right?" Ann came closer and reached one hand out to smooth Ari's hair. "Dr. Bohnes didn't know how long you'd been asleep on the floor in the storeroom, but she didn't think it was too long."

Just all afternoon, Ari thought. *She'd go wild if I told her I fell asleep for hours and that I had nightmares every minute and then I heard this strange song. Not to mention the eye. What's happening to me? Did the accident scramble my brains and my legs, both?* Aloud, she merely said, "I'm fine, Ann." She set the knives, forks, and spoons in place and sat down at the table.

"Well, we're not." Frank closed the red book with a thump. There were deep purple smudges beneath his tired eyes. He rubbed the back of his hand over his mouth. "We're broke."

Ari looked down at her plate. Ann put a ladle full of macaroni and cheese in the center. The yellow cheese oozed onto a blue lady with a sweet, sad expression. Frank thumped heavily across the wooden floor and sat at Ari's right. Ann took her place across from her. Ari said, "We have to lease Chase, then. There's no way out."

"I'm sorry, Ari, I really am. But the money we can get from Mr. Carmichael is money to feed the other animals." He smiled, a tired, sad smile. "And us, of course." He reached over and touched her sleeve lightly. "I know you mind. I know you mind a lot."

"They're going to take him away? To another trainer?"

Neither Ann nor Frank said anything. It was,

Ari thought with a sudden spurt of rage, because they were too cowardly.

"Don't look like that," Frank said nervously. "If there was any other way, you know we'd take it."

"You could sell that necklace Lincoln had around his neck." Ari set her fork carefully across her plate. Then she drew the fine chain over her head and held the ruby up. It caught the firelight. Its glow was like the heart of the fire itself.

Ann looked away, as if the sight of the jewel were too much to bear. Frank put his hands before his eyes.

"No!" Ann's voice was hoarse. "You must never, ever let that out of your sight. Do you understand?" She leaned forward. Her breath smelled of peppermint.

"We could sell it," Ari said. "Where's it from, anyway? And what was a valuable thing like this doing around Linc's neck?"

"We don't know," Frank said uneasily. He cast a sidelong glance at Lincoln, curled as usual at Ari's feet. "But we can't sell it. You can't sell it."

"If it's mine, I can." Ari twirled the necklace carelessly around one finger.

Horror spread over Frank's face slowly like a stain spreading in water. "Put it away," he said in the grimmest voice she had ever heard from him. "And we'll have no more talk of that, Ari. Do you understand?"

"Frank," Ann said in a low voice. "Maybe

she's right. Maybe here, it doesn't matter. After all, here he's a horse. He doesn't look anything like . . ."

"What doesn't matter?" Ari asked. "And he doesn't look like what?"

"Nothing." Frank sighed. "Nothing. It's safer for you not to know. Eat your dinner, Ari. Please. And don't think about it anymore."

"You won't change your mind? About Chase?"

"I can't, Ari. I'm sorry."

Ari drew the necklace back over her head. She tucked the ruby inside her shirt next to her heart.

Ari helped with the dishes and went up to bed early. She kissed Ann and Frank good night and smiled when Ann drew back in surprise at the intensity of her hug. She whistled lightly at Lincoln. The big dog uncurled himself from the corner and padded up the stairs after her.

She went into her room and snapped on the light. It was strange, she thought. She only remembered three months of being in this room. She had no memory of what her bedroom had been like before. But she felt so cozy here; her room "before" (as she thought of the time when she had two whole legs) must have been a lot like this one. Pale green walls, and a flowered bedspread to match. White wicker dresser and nightstand. The desk where she'd thought she'd do homework when she started school in the fall. Except, according to Ann and Dr.

Bohnes, she wouldn't be starting school at all. Well, she could have done the homework Dr. Bohnes would have given her here. If she was going to stay.

"I can't, Linc. I can't stay here and let Chase go to someone else." The horse wouldn't stand for it. And when Chase didn't want to do something — the only person to stop him was Ari herself. If she didn't take him away in the morning, terrible things would happen. Mr. Carmichael meant his threat. If Chase did hurt Lori — and the way Lori rode, he would hurt Lori, even if he didn't mean to — Ari had heard Mr. Carmichael say it:

Chase would be shot.

Ari stripped off her breeches and T-shirt, then grabbed her pajamas. She put one bare leg into the bottoms and stopped, looking at the twisted muscle, the scars that the accident had left. She finished putting her nightclothes on and got into bed. She switched the bedside lamp off, then heard Linc settle heavily onto the rug at the side of the bed. She slept.

And as she slept, she dreamed.

12

The moon sailed high and white over Glacier River Farm. It shone through Ari's open window and turned the patchwork on her quilt to pale shadows. To Linc, who lay beside Ari's bed, the moon was known as the Silver Traveler. He watched it now, head on forepaws, dark eyes shining, as it bobbed along the river of sky until it reached the giant pines that guarded the forest. Then the Silver Traveler floated there, as if caught in the net of the trees.

Lincoln raised his head, eyes suddenly alert. A ray of moonlight passed through the window and touched Ari's sleeping form. She stirred in her sleep and sighed.

The moonlight grew stronger, harder, turning from heavenly light to earthly substance, until a solid arch appeared. One end rested at the foot of Ari's bed. The other rose to the Silver Traveler at the top of the pines. There was a distant sound of bells, as if some celestial harness jingled. A light brighter than the moon appeared at the top of the arch and moved swiftly down the path. The jingling of the harness bells grew sweeter, not louder.

Lincoln whined, deep in his throat.

The bright light stopped at the window's ledge, as if hesitating to enter or considering where to go. Then it passed into Ari's bedroom and stopped at the arch's end.

Lincoln rose to his feet. The light dimmed for a second, or perhaps less, then flowered to a brilliant rose. A unicorn stood in the center, her horn a crystal spear, her coat a burnished violet. Her white mane flowed like spun silver, reaching her knees, covering her withers, so that she appeared to be wrapped in moonlight.

Atalanta. Goddess to All the Animals. Atalanta, the Bearer of Legends and the Keeper of Stories. The Dreamspeaker! She had come! Lincoln lowered his head and sighed, contented.

"And, you," she said to the dog, a steely note in her silvery voice. "Who are you, dog?"

Linc raised his eyes at her and thumped his tail.

"What? You cannot speak? Or will not?"

Linc whined, then rolled over on his back, white belly exposed to the unicorn's sharp horn.

Atalanta tilted her head to one side, considering the collie. Whatever had sent him seemed to bear the Princess no ill will. And there were limits to what she would be allowed to do. She, too, sighed deeply. She gazed at the sleeping Ari, her eyes a tender purple. She moved nearer, hovering over the bed, carried by the arch of moonlight. Gently, she lowered her crystal horn until the very tip touched the ruby at Ari's throat. The jewel warmed slowly to a deep red flame.

"I will tell you the Story, little one," Atalanta said in her gentle voice. "But you must come to me to hear it."

Ari stirred and murmured in her sleep. The ruby necklace shimmered as she turned.

"If you come to me, Ari, I may tell you everything."

"Mother?" Ari said sleepily. "No. Where are you? Who are you?"

"Ah, Ari, I live where the Arch meets the Imperial River. That is my home. But I will meet you elsewhere, if you will come."

"It isn't you, Mother, is it?" Ari's eyes fluttered. She yawned. Atalanta raised her head. As soon as her horn left the jewel, the fiery light in it died away. The silver Arch beneath her hooves began to dim.

"Remember, Ari. Come to me. Because you love the Sunchaser. Because you love me. Ari, the most important thing of all? You must use the jewel to save the Sunchaser. It is his, and his alone. Help him! He cannot be who he is without it!" She turned and began to walk the arch to go back to the Silver Traveler in the sky. She left the scent of flowers behind her.

When Ari came fully awake, the only memento of Atalanta's visit was a faint silver shimmer in the air and a smell of roses. But that could have been only the moonlight and the air from the open window.

"Linc!" Ari sat up in bed. She rubbed her eyes and yawned again. She reached over the side of the bed to the floor, her hand fumbling for the dog. She felt the silken triangle of his head and then his warm tongue on her fingers. She scratched his ears a little, the way he liked best, then swung her feet onto the floor and switched on the bedside light. "I had the strangest dream," she said. He looked back at her, tongue hanging out, a grin on his face.

"You silly dog." She bent over and hugged him. "It was a nice dream," she said quietly into his ear. "A beautiful dream." She inhaled happily. "I believe I can still smell the flowers from that dream, Linc. Do you know what I saw?"

I do, his eyes seemed to say.

"Of course you don't, silly. So I'll tell you. But we have to tell Chase first. Okay?"

Lincoln cocked his head. Ari pulled on a heavy sweater and prepared to tiptoe as quietly as possible down the stairs and out to the barn. "But first," she whispered to the dog, "I'm going to put this in a really safe place." She tucked the ruby necklace carefully into her top drawer, under a pile of riding socks. "Just imagine what would happen if I lost it now!"

Linc followed her out of the house and to the back of the clinic, where Chase was stabled with Max the buckskin for company. Max stirred as she approached, and nickered. Ari smiled to herself. Hoping for a handout. She slipped through the fence rails and walked to her horse. Chase stood dreaming his own dreams. She slid her hand along his satiny sides. He turned to her with a look of surprise.

Ari wrapped her arms around his neck and whispered in his ear. "I dreamed of a magical creature. A unicorn. And it was so funny, Chase. I just know I've had this dream before." She frowned to herself. "Or maybe it wasn't a dream. Maybe it was from my time before the accident." She laughed. "Except there aren't any unicorns, are there, Chase?"

He blew out once.

Ari rubbed his ears tenderly, her expression thoughtful. "You know, Chase, I was getting just a little bit scared to take you and Linc away from here. I was thinking we could leave the farm here and find another farm, where they don't know us. I could work for our room and board, cleaning stalls and grooming the horses, and maybe we could sleep in the hayloft. It would be warm there, even in winter."

Chase whinnied. Ari knew what that whinny meant. "You think that's a bad idea? It has its disadvantages. Frank would plaster my photograph all over the television stations, and whoever took us in would take us right back. That is, if we didn't get hurt by some horrible person first. But you know — that dream gave me a fabulous idea."

Chase's eyes were mysterious in the dark of the barn. Ari rubbed his muzzle affectionately. "I'm going to start by talking nicely to Lori and her father in the morning. She can't possibly want a horse that doesn't want her. Once she sees that he'll never listen to another trainer, she's got to give it up." She hugged Chase hard. "I know. You think that she and her father are so selfish, they'll never let you go. I've thought about how to fix that, too." She frowned. "I've been thinking about money. Lori and her father like money more than anything, I think. Well, I've had an absolute brainstorm. I'm going to use the jewel to save you! That's what came to me in the dream. I think. Anyway, I'm going to get Dr. Bohnes to sell the ruby necklace for me! She's the only one who will really understand about you and me. And she knows that the necklace is mine to sell. She won't feel as *responsible* as Ann does." She laughed. "And that necklace has to be worth a huge amount. I'll give part of the cash to Lori and her father in return for breaking that lease agreement. The other part of the cash will pay off the debts we've got. This is going to work, Chase. I just know it will."

Ari fed him a handful of sweet feed, then limped barefooted through the damp grass and back into her room. She fell asleep and dreamed no more dreams.

13

Ari was up with the sun. She dressed quickly. There is always more work than time to do it in on a horse farm. Ari felt guilty about missing her assigned chores from the day before. So she was determined to do twice as much work this morning. She owed it to Ann and Frank. She'd tried to thank Frank once. He'd given her the warmest smile she'd ever seen. "It's nothing, mila . . . my dear. We'd spend twice as much if we had to."

"But it doesn't mean they should," she said to Linc. The jewel was still in her sock drawer. She drew it out and held it tight for a moment. How much was it worth? A hundred thousand dollars? She didn't know. But Dr. Bohnes would. She tucked it carefully away again. She wore her blue denim shirt and her breeches and patted her breast pocket to make sure that the stones she'd found the day before were still safely there. Maybe she'd find more of them today. And maybe, like the ruby necklace, they'd be worth some money. Heck! She could be rich and not even know it!

The morning air was fresh, the sun a narrow orange slice above the eastern horizon. Ari was happy. Her legs were achy this morning, but not too cramped. With luck, she'd have all her problems solved by lunchtime. Dr. Bohnes would sell the ruby necklace for a pile of money. Lori and her father would want the money instead of Chase. And all the bills would be paid off. She was sure of it.

Maybe she and the great stallion could take a long ride this afternoon!

She fed and watered all the horses — taking care of Chase first. Then she turned all the horses in the big barn out to pasture and began to clean the stalls. Lincoln helped her by staying out of the way.

Mucking out was hard work, but Ari enjoyed it. She worked hard this morning. She wanted to get every chore finished before breakfast. Lori had scheduled a lesson on Chase at nine o'clock, and so far she hadn't canceled it.

Ari used a large plastic manure fork that let her lift the piles neatly into the manure wagon. After the piles were dumped, she turned the fork over, pointy side down, and raked the sawdust bedding away from the damp spots. The air dried out the dirt floor.

Then she raked all the sawdust neatly to the sides of all the stalls and put the manure fork away.

She surveyed her work with satisfaction. She was a heck of a good barn rat, if she said so herself. She'd be employable anywhere. "Because," she reminded Linc, "you just never know when you're going to need a good job. You know? I can see it all. I'll have a job, a little money in the bank, and life will be wonderful. And all because of that necklace."

She checked the large clock over the barn office door. It was seven-forty-five. She had just enough time before breakfast to drive the tractor and wagon out to the manure pile and dump it.

She settled into the tractor seat, shifted the gear into drive, and drove slowly out of the barn. She put on the brake when she saw the Carmichaels' big red Cadillac pull into the parking lot. A pickup truck pulling a horse trailer came into the lot right behind them.

She took a deep breath. They were early. Way too early.

Mr. Carmichael got out of the car. He looked fatter and angrier than ever. Lori jumped out of the passenger side. She was wearing a new pair of breeches and shiny new paddock boots. The Cadillac had turned up dust when Mr. Carmichael pulled in. It settled on Lori's boots. She scowled, bent over, and fussily wiped them off. The driver of the pickup truck got out, too. Ari knew him. She'd seen him with his students at a farm horse show just two weeks ago. David Greer Smith. So that was the trainer the Carmichaels had hired with all their money. And he was a good trainer, too.

Mr. Carmichael waved his arms and jabbered at Mr. Smith. Lori stood next to her father, arms folded, the scowl still on her face. Suddenly, the three of them turned and walked off to the clinic, where Chase still stood in the paddock. Ari's heart quickened. How did the Carmichaels know where to find Chase? His usual stall was in the front of the barn. Who told them where Chase was?

"Morning, Ari."

Ari jumped. "Frank! Sorry. I didn't hear you come up."

He put his hand on her shoulder. "You did a lot of work this morning."

"Frank, what are they doing here so early?"

"The Carmichaels?" He turned and looked after them. The trainer walked in front of the other two. He was swinging a long lead line in one hand. "Smith called about half an hour ago. You were just starting to muck out. Said they wanted to take Chase bright and early. It's a long ride to his new stable, I guess."

"But you *can't*!" Ari burst out.

"He said they'd sue us if we didn't let him take Chase to a new stable! We'd lose everything, Ari. And our first duty is to you. Ann and I talked and talked about it this morning. We have no choice! This guy's backed us into a corner."

Ari remained calm. "I have this plan. We'll get lots of money, Frank. Truly we will. You have to stop them."

His hand lightened on her shoulder. "Honey, I just ca —"

"Won't, you mean," Ari said furiously. She ran to the clinic, Lincoln barking at her heels. She could hear Frank shout, "Stop! Stop!" She didn't care.

By the time she reached the paddock, she was out of breath. David Greer Smith was a tall man in cowboy boots, jeans, and a denim jacket. He was already inside the fence. Chase was backed into one corner. The stallion looked at the trainer out of the corner of his eye. Ari couldn't read Chase's expression. But she didn't think he was happy. Not upset, yet, she thought. Just curious. And a little annoyed.

"Sir!" she called out.

The trainer turned around. He had a nice face, Ari thought. But nice or not, he wasn't going to get her horse.

"What are you doing here?" Lori demanded.

"What are you doing here?" Ari shot back. "I've come to tell you the deal's off."

The door to the clinic opened and Dr. Bohnes came out. She was wearing a plastic rain hat and rubber boots over a screaming-loud green shirt and black pants. She looked ridiculous, but Ari was happy to see her. "Well," Dr. Bohnes said. She raised her scraggly white eyebrows to her hairline. "What's going on here?"

"We've come to get the horse, as agreed," Mr. Carmichael said in a curt way. "Get this kid out of the way, Frank. She could get hurt."

Ari bit her lip. She didn't have much time. She had to get to Dr. Bohnes alone — with no one else around. She knew Dr. Bohnes would help her sell the necklace. But how could she get all these people out of here?

She looked at Chase. The trainer was advancing on him, the lead line held behind his back. Chase snorted and flung his head up. Then he backed away. The trainer made soft clucking noises with his tongue. Chase danced a little on the tips of his hooves. When the trainer got close, the horse jumped away, just out of reach.

"Good," Ari said under her breath. Then aloud, "Dr. Bohnes?"

"What is it, my dear?"

"Could I talk to you? For just a second?"

"Whoa!" The trainer roared.

Everybody jumped. Except for Chase, who danced away again, just out of reach. The trainer's face was getting red.

"Maybe now's not the time, dear." Dr. Bohnes tied the plastic rain hat more firmly on her white hair. Frank looked up at the sky, which was clear and cloudless, but he didn't say anything. Ari ignored them both. Fine. So the little vet wouldn't help her. She'd just have to help herself. Get Chase away from here, just for a few hours, while she tried to settle things. Quietly, she moved away from the Carmichaels and the others and up to the paddock fence. Chase rolled his eye at her. She lifted her hand to make him whoa.

He stopped obediently at her signal.

"Jeez," said the trainer. He spat on the ground in a disgusted way. Then he grabbed Chase's halter and snapped the lead line onto the ring under his chin.

Ari moved her hand sideways, in a swift, abrupt motion. Chase jerked sharply to the left. The lead line tore out of the surprised trainer's hands. Ari raised her palm. Chase reared, forelegs pawing the air. He was having a good time.

The trainer swore angrily, leaped in the air, and grabbed the lead line. He gave one powerful tug on the line and jerked the horse forward. Then he grabbed the free end of the line and swung it viciously at the stallion's face. The horse roared in anger.

"NO!" Ari said.

I will trample you, little man!

Ari gasped. There it was again. Chase's voice. In her head. As though he was speaking to her. She jumped onto the fence and clung to the top board, her fingers digging into the rough wood. Chase was furious at the insult of the blow. He pawed at the

106

ground, clouds of dirt flying from beneath his iron hooves. The trainer backed up, his face a mask of fear. Chase whinnied, a high, trumpeting challenge.

Get him out of here, milady. Or he will die!

"Sir!" Ari called. "Please! Sir! Just back up. Please just back up. Don't make him any madder."

OUT! shouted the voice in her head.

"You stop, Chase," she ordered aloud.

For a breathless moment, she wasn't sure it would work. It was crazy anyway, a part of her brain whispered. Talking to your horse?

Chase reared once more, black against the bright blue sky and the brilliant sun. Then he came to earth with a crash and stood still.

"You made him do that!" Lori shrieked. "You made him run away from the trainer. Daddy, I'm *telling* you, if we can just get him away from her, that horse will be just fine. She's just jealous, Daddy, because he likes me better or he would if he got half a chance!" Furious, she shoved her elbow into Ari's stomach. Ari fell backward with a gasp. There was a swirl of coffee-colored fur, a snarl, a scream. Linc jumped across her and barreled full tilt into Lori. He knocked her facedown, then settled all his eighty pounds right onto her back. Lori drummed her heels and yelled, but the big dog didn't turn a hair.

"That's enough out of everyone," Dr. Bohnes said briskly. To the trainer she said, "You, come out of that paddock and talk to me like a sensible man. And you," she turned to Mr. Carmichael, "pick up

107

that spoiled little brat of yours and come into my office. All of you. You, too, Frank. We're going to settle this once and for all." She turned her back, marched into the clinic, and left the door wide open.

The trainer picked up his hat, dusted it off, and settled it firmly on his head. "I'll tell you what that horse needs," he said to no one in particular. "He needs a good whipping." He followed Dr. Bohnes into her office.

"Ari!" Frank tugged her arm. "Ari? Can you get that darn dog off of Ms. Carmichael?"

Ari turned around and bit her lip to keep from laughing. Mr. Carmichael was tugging like anything at the big collie's thick ruff. Linc wasn't budging. He sat on Lori's backside with a grin on his face, completely ignoring the infuriated man. Ari whistled. Linc pricked up his ears, hopped off Lori, and walked over to Ari, his tail wagging happily.

Lori picked herself up. Her new boots were smudged and her perfect blond hair didn't look anywhere near perfect anymore. Her face was redder than her father's.

"You two stay here," Mr. Carmichael ordered. "Come on, Frank. We'll settle this with the old bat inside."

"She is not," Ari said clearly, "an old bat."

"Just shut up," Lori muttered.

"Both of you keep quiet. Please?" Frank said. "I'll be with you in a minute, Mr. Carmichael." He waited until the other man had disappeared into Dr.

108

Bohnes's office. Then he came over to Ari and crouched in front of her. "Ari," he said.

"Yes, Frank?"

"You've got to let the horse go."

Ari shook her head. "I'm going to sell that necklace. Dr. Bohnes will do it for me."

"No, she won't. She can't."

"It's mine, isn't it?"

He hesitated. "Well, yes."

"Then I can sell it."

"Even if you do sell it, Ari, the Carmichaels don't have to take the money back. We have a contract." His thin face was lined with worry and distress. "Do you know what that means?"

"It means you signed my horse away."

"I signed your horse away. But it's just for a year. And then he'll be home, I promise." He stood up and ran his hands through his hair. Ari suddenly felt very sorry for him. "My gosh, this sure got mixed up," he said under his breath. "You two wait right here. I'll be back in a few minutes."

Ari watched as he went into the clinic and shut the door. Lori stood a little apart from her, arms folded defiantly over her chest. Finally she said, "That stupid dog of yours should be shot, too."

Ari decided not to respond to this. Lori was a horrible mess of a human being, and that was that. There wasn't a thing she could say to her. The best thing was to totally ignore her.

She gathered her long hair up into a knot,

fished a rubber band out of her jeans pocket, and wound it into a ponytail. Then she went into the paddock.

"Where are you going?"

"None of your business," Ari said shortly. She took the lead line the trainer had left in the dust and clipped it on the left ring of Chase's halter. Then she tied the free end to the ring on the other side. She looked up at her horse. Her legs were still too mangled to jump on him from the ground. She'd have to get a box. "You stand," she said softly. She left him there, still as a statue and as good as gold.

"I'm getting a step stool from the shed!" she said loudly.

Lori shrugged: *Who cares?*

Once in the shed, Ari peeked out. Lori was staring after her, but she was pretty sure she couldn't see what she was doing. She just hoped that Dr. Bohnes hadn't gotten a sudden (and rare) cleaning fit. The old vet hadn't. The windows were still as filthy as ever. Ari wrote on the dirty pane with one finger:

Sell the "DOG LEASH" in my sock drawer!

PLEASE!

Love, Ari.

"And I hope," Ari said fiercely to herself, "she remembers how the necklace came here. Linc was wearing it around his neck."

Then she picked up the step stool and marched out of the shed. She set it on the ground next to Chase.

"What are you *doing*?" Lori demanded.

"Leaving," Ari said briefly. She leaped neatly onto the stallion's back and settled her long legs just behind his withers. His chest and barrel were so powerful that the spot between them made a perfect place to keep a good grip. She squeezed her left leg, and he responded by turning in a circle. Max, the buckskin gave a startled squeal and jumped out of the way.

Ari spread the makeshift reins wide, tapped both heels lightly against his sides, and he backed up a few steps. Then she gathered the lead line in, tapped more firmly, and he sprang forward. They flew up and over the fence.

"You can't do that!" Lori screamed. "You come back here!"

"Linc!" Ari called. "Come on, boy!"

But Lori moved with astonishing speed. She grabbed the dog's ruff with both hands and held on. Linc wriggled in her grip. He looked at her. Ari looked back. Lori wasn't about to let go, unless Linc bit her. And Linc would bite only if she gave him permission. "Linc!" she called. "You find me when you can. Got that? Find me."

He barked. Ari prayed that he did understand. That, like Chase, when emotions were high he could somehow figure out what she needed.

She raised a hand in farewell and galloped Chase into the woods.

14

Atalanta splashed one cloven hoof in the water and watched the ripples drift away. She stood under a sapphire willow tree at the edge of the Imperial River, watching the world of Glacier River Farm in the magic waters of the Watching Pool. The vision was of Arianna and the Sunchaser fleeing the only security they had.

The willow branches dropped gracefully into the crystal-clear stream. Whenever a breeze came up, blossoms fell, blurring the images of Arianna and the Sunchaser. Then the flowers swirled away like little blue boats carried on the current. Sapphire willows grew only in the Valley of the Unicorns, as far as Atalanta knew. And Atalanta was the wisest unicorn in the Celestial Valley herd.

She raised her head and looked across the fields to rest her eyes from the visions. It had been a long, long night. A month had come and gone, and the Shifter's Moon was back. There'd been no attack from the Shifter — at least not yet. And Atalanta had walked the Path from the Moon and across the Gap to warn Arianna in a dream. But there were still three nights left of the Shifter's Moon, when her personal magic would not work — and Arianna was racing toward — what?

Atalanta sighed. Her crystal horn scattered splintered light on the grass.

It was so beautiful, her world! Unicorns stood peacefully throughout the Celestial Valley, as bright as the colors of the rainbow: Blue, scarlet, bronze, emerald, each a jewel of light in the already light-filled land. A sunstruck golden unicorn — brighter than the others — grazed on the hillside at Valley's end. Numinor, the Golden One.

All this beauty. All this could pass away in the next few days.

"What news at Glacier River?" Tobiano marched heavily through the grass, curious as always about matters that didn't concern him.

Atalanta nodded her greetings. The black-and-white-spotted unicorn was as rude as he was nosy. Atalanta's clear violet eyes softened with amusement. Tobiano had a good heart, in spite of himself. "Come and see."

He came and stood by her. Together, they watched Arianna and the Sunchaser take the paddock fence and gallop to freedom in the woods. The collie wasn't with them.

"She isn't wearing the jewel?" Tobiano asked.

Atalanta closed her eyes for a long moment. "No," she said sadly. "She is not wearing the jewel. And the dog isn't there. I still don't know what to make of the dog, Toby."

"Huh!" Tobiano's horn was short, but the noise he made through it was loud and brassy enough for a unicorn with a much longer one. "And what are you going to do about that?"

"I did what I could, Toby." She lifted her head and looked at him. Her silvery mane stirred in the soft breeze. "I have already broken the laws of our kind by visiting her on that side of the Gap. That's all I could do. I can't tell her the rest. Not yet. Not unless she crosses the Gap. And if she crosses the Gap, she will be in grave, grave danger. . . . We have no power over the humans at Glacier River, other than the power of dreams. What more could I do?"

Toby looked cross. "You could have told her straight out what's going on," he grumped. "I would have."

"Perhaps," Atalanta said, with a slight edge to her soft voice, "that is why I am Dreamspeaker and you are not. The laws are there for a reason."

"Huh!" Toby said again. "If you ask me —"

"Well, I haven't asked you," Atalanta said, reasonably enough.

"Certain unicorns I know ought to do a little more than just stand around looking into the Watching Pool when there's this much trouble afoot."

114

"If she crosses the Gap, I can do a little more than just visit her, Toby. But she has to cross first. You know that."

"Blah, blah," he said grouchily.

A slight frown appeared between Atalanta's violet eyes. Toby ducked his head, embarrassed. Apparently even he had limits to his rudeness. He muttered a quick, "Sorry!" Then, "We're all doin' our best. I mean, I know you're doin' your best. You lemme know if I can help."

She looked at him steadily. "Would you be willing to walk the Path from the Moon with me to join them? Into Balinor? I have a job for you. Your colors are very . . . usual, Toby. With a little care, you could look just like a unicorn of Balinor. We can disguise your jewel. If you were clever, and I know you can be, no one would guess that you are a celestial unicorn."

Toby looked as if he didn't know whether this was a compliment or not.

"It is very important," Atalanta assured him. "I need to have you tell me what's going on in Balinor. I see only what I ask to see in the Watching Pool. And, Toby, if I don't know what to ask, we could all be in very serious trouble. I want you to walk among the unicorns of Balinor as one of them and tell me of events that I do not know." She leaned close to him and bent her head to his ear. "There is no one else in the herd that could do it."

Toby rubbed his black-and-white horn

against the trunk of the sapphire willow tree. He brought his left hind hoof up and scratched his left ear. He yawned carelessly, as if what Atalanta said had been an ordinary, everyday kind of thing. Instead of what it really was. A challenge. An adventure. Leave the Celestial Valley? Walk the Path from the Moon to the earth below? He, Tobiano, the rudest unicorn in the celestial herd? A chance to be . . . a hero?

Atalanta may have smiled a little. It was hard to tell. She said in her gentle voice, "I'd have to check with Numinor, the Golden One, of course. But he would allow you to leave the herd. If you are willing to go."

Toby hummed a careless little tune through his horn to hide his excitement and said, "Sure. Heck. Why not?" And he turned and marched off, rolling through the meadow like a little barrel.

Atalanta turned back to the Watching Pool and watched as Arianna tried to lose herself and her horse in the woods outside Glacier River Farm. She leaned closer to the water, her silvery mane trailing in the starflowers on the bank . . . and watched.

15

✤

Ari raced along, her body swaying comfortably. Chase's hand gallop was smooth and swift. She felt as if she wasn't really sitting on his great bronze back, it was as if she were floating. She kept a sharp lookout for woodchuck holes and stones. The stallion was agile and quick, but at this speed even he could trip and fall. She would go to the cave created by the long-ago glaciers in their path to the sea. The cave in the south pasture. Near the meadow where she'd found the first of the strange spiral stones. The south pasture was large enough to hide Chase and her during the day.

It called to her now, stronger than ever.

She shook her head, as if to free it from dreams. Linc knew where the cave was. As soon as he got away from Lori and her father, he would find them. So it was a sensible thing to do.

Wasn't it?

She pulled Chase to a half-halt at the edge of the south pasture. It was peaceful under the sun, the uncut hay shifting slightly with the breeze. The cave lay on the far side. The entrance was concealed because the meadow dropped off to a deep ravine, but she could see it with her mind's eye, as clear as anything.

Ari guided Chase through the grass with her knees, the lead line loose over his neck. She listened carefully. Were there shouts in the distance? And was that the sound of another horse?

She felt Chase tense between her knees. His head came up. He whinnied, the call of a stallion to a member of the herd. Someone was after them. Ari leaned over his neck and whispered urgently, "Hush. Hush now, Chase."

She urged him to a swift trot. They reached the meadow's edge, and she slid to the ground. She walked carefully down the slope to the cave, urging the horse along with small murmurs of encouragement. He slid, caught himself, then flattened his ears. This meant he was cross with her, and despite the urgency of her search for the cave, Ari felt laughter bubble up in her throat. "Well, I'm sorry," she muttered. "I know you don't like it when the footing's rough. But this is an emergency, Chase."

He snorted and even seemed to nod his head. Ari wondered again about her ability to catch his thoughts. Was it true that he could speak with

118

her in moments of great stress? Or was it just her imagination?

"There it is, Chase. The cave." She pulled on the lead line. He caught sight of the dark entrance, barely taller that his head. He balked, pulling her backward.

"No, Chase." She kept her voice low, but put all the urgency she could into it. "I know you don't like small, dark places. No horse does. But we have to hide. Just for a while." She stopped herself and listened hard.

Arianna! That whisper on the breeze! She rubbed her hands through her hair. Was the voice coming from the cave?

Ari cocked her head. The voice — if it had been a voice — faded with the wind. And now there was no doubt about it. There was a horse coming through the woods after them. Somewhere north of where they were now, which meant it or they were coming from the farm itself. "Come on, Chase." She tugged at the lead line. Chase backed up, swinging his head back and forth, back and forth. He dug his hind hooves into the ground and pulled away. So it was serious then, his refusal to go into that deep dark place. She loosened the line; Dr. Bohnes always said in a tug-of-war between a fourteen-hundred-pound horse and a one-hundred-and-three-pound human, it should be obvious who would win.

119

She made her voice firm and low. "Please, Chase. *Please*. For me."

The faraway hoofbeats grew nearer. Then stopped. Good. He or she or whoever was up there wasn't sure which way to go. But she had so little time!

Ari quickly freed the makeshift reins from the knot she'd made and turned the rope into a lead line again. She clipped the line to the ring in Chase's halter and backed herself into the cave, not pulling, just letting him stand. She would let him make his own decision. "See, Chase. Come on, boy. Walk in. It's just a nice hiding place. There's nothing in here."

She stopped herself in midsentence. There *was* something in here. She could feel it. And there was an odor. Faint. Horrible. Just like the stink she had run into the day before, in the meadow and then again in the vet's room. Still holding the lead line, she turned and searched the darkness with her eyes. It had rock walls and a dirt and gravel floor. There was slight trickle of damp from an underground water source.

Was that a low buzzing? A whine? Flies, black flies? Yes! She could just make out a mass of them against the north wall. No wonder Chase didn't want to come in. Horses hated black flies. She backstepped out into daylight. If she soothed him, explained to him, maybe she could ride him in.

Chase's ears pricked forward and he turned his head, listening to something behind him. There was a familiar scrabbling through the brush above. Lincoln poked his head over the lip of the rise and looked down on them. He had escaped the Carmichaels! He barked once. Ari knew that bark: It was a warning. The dog bounded down the slope. He came directly to her, bumped her knee with his head, then whirled and faced the rise. He barked again, and again Ari knew what it meant: Stay away! *Stay away!*

The thrumming of hooves grew nearer. Ari took a deep breath. She would face them, whoever they were. She heard a horse breathing hard and heavy, and a grunt from the animal as the rider pulled him up. His feet scrabbled in the gravel at the lip of the rise, just as Chase's had done. Then Max, the buckskin, fell over the edge. He slid down on his haunches. The rider on his back pulled hard on the reins. The gelding's mouth gaped wide and he twisted his head with the effort to get away from the bit.

Horse and rider tumbled straight toward them. Lincoln threw himself in front of Ari, trying to protect her. Still holding the lead line, Ari leaped backward into the cave. Max made a massive effort to avoid sliding into them. He gave a great heave with his front legs. The rider flew off and crashed into Chase. The stallion leaped forward, startled at the impact. His great chest smashed into Ari. She fell flat on her back, her head hitting the stone wall.

121

There was an immense, terrifying buzz of a million flies.

She heard Lincoln's snarl of rage.

There was a flash of bright violet, the scent of flowers.

And then . . . she heard nothing at all.

16

A̓ri woke up. She had wakened like this once before. After the accident. After the terrible crash that had twisted her legs and wiped her memory as clean as a blackboard eraser.

But then, she had awakened to pain worse than fire. Now she woke to sky that was a different blue from any blue she had seen before. To the smells of a forest that wasn't pine — but what?

Cautiously, she sat up. The ache in her legs was familiar: a dull throb in her calves where the scars were, an ache in her right knee. No different, then. No new injuries.

She sighed in relief. A wave of dizziness swept over her and she fell on her back. She fought the blackness. Chase! Where was Chase? A cold nose poked her neck, a warm tongue licked her cheek. She smiled gratefully and wound her hands in Lincoln's ruff. He stepped back and she held on to pull herself upright again. She blinked the dizziness away and looked. Chase stood near. So near that she reached out one hand and steadied herself against his iron-muscled foreleg. He bent his head and whiffed gently into her hair. She got up and dusted off her breeches.

Are you all right, milady?

His voice in her head! Tentatively, she spoke to him. "Chase? Is that you? Or am I dreaming?" She bit her lip and said to herself more than to the others, "Or maybe I'm crazy? The doctors told me they weren't sure why my memory's gone. Maybe I'm just plain nuts."

Chase looked back at her. The nice little wrinkles over each eye were sharply cut with worry. His nostrils flared red and his lower lip was tightly closed. She knew he was upset. She stroked his neck, then quickly checked him over. She remembered falling down, the horse and the dog rolling after her. If either one were hurt, she'd have to run back to the farm for help.

I have no hurt, no wound. But she may be injured. Go to her.

"She? Who?" A groan answered her. Ari looked around.

And she felt as if a giant hand squeezed all the breath out of her. Wherever Ari was, she wasn't at Glacier River Farm anymore.

The sky she'd wakened to not moments before was a purple-blue, unlike any she'd seen before.

She was in a meadow. At least, she was pretty sure it was a meadow. The grass was thick, knee-high, and of a bluish-green that reminded her more of water than anything else. The broad-bladed blue-green grass was as thick and uniform as a carpet.

The meadow itself was an irregularly shaped circle surrounded by dense trees. But the trees weren't any more normal than the grass or the sky. They were tall, with thickly gnarled branches that bent and twisted.

Had she been here before? A second groan, louder than the first, jerked her back to her companions. Lincoln, his tail waving, danced through the strange thick-bladed grass and bent his head to look at whatever was lying there. Ari hesitated. Should she run away?

"I will not," she said aloud. Chase snorted in approval. She cautiously approached Lincoln and whatever he was looking at. She wished she had a heavy branch.

The third groan made Ari stand up straight and march over to the hump in the grass. She knew that voice. And she was well acquainted with the crossness in it. She put her hands on her hips and looked down. "Lori Carmichael! What are you doing here?"

Lori's hair was tangled with bits of twigs and gravel. She wasn't hurt: Ari saw that right away. She was sitting cross-legged, with her head on her knees. And that last groan was exasperated, angry

125

even, but not wounded. The blond girl blinked up at her. Her face was scratched and muddy. "What have you done now?" she grumbled.

"What have I done? You were the one who came chasing after me. And Max. Poor Max. You rode him too hard, as you always do. When you came crashing down that . . ."

"He *slipped,*" Lori said furiously. "Can I help it if that dumb horse slipped!?"

Chase walked gracefully through the grass and stood next to Ari, watching Lori with courteous interest. Lori glared at him and got to her feet. Ari suppressed a giggle. Lori's breeches were torn right across the seat. And her underwear was green with little flowers on it.

"What did you do with him?" Lori demanded in a nasty voice.

"With Max, you mean?"

"With Max, you mean?" Lori mimicked furiously. "Who else, stupid? Godzilla? If you think I'm walking back to the farm all bumped up like this, you've got another think coming."

Chase lowered his head and nudged Ari gently. *He did not cross the Gap with us.*

"Gap?" Ari put her hand on Chase's mane. It was silky under her hand. "Chase, what's the . . . Gap?"

I do not . . . I do not . . . recall.

"What are you doing now! Talking to your horse? Great. Just *great.* I told Daddy that accident made you loony, and I was right." Lori took a couple of steps toward them, then looked down to shove Lincoln out of the way. He growled, deep in his throat, but moved aside.

Lori looked around angrily, then gasped. Her face turned white. For the first time she seemed to realize that she — they — were in a place so strange it might have been another planet. "What's going on here?" Her voice quivered. She looked at the trees, with their bizarre branches bent and curled like hair after a bad perm. She glanced up at the purple-blue sky and looked past the trees to the horizon beyond. She flushed bright red and pointed, her eyes so wide Ari could see the whites all around them. "Ari! Ari! *What is that?*"

Ari shaded her eyes with her hands and looked at the sun. It was in the same position in the sky it had been at home, about halfway between the eastern horizon and straight overhead. Which meant Lori was pointing west. Ari wheeled around slowly, almost afraid to look beyond the trees. "Why, it's a village!" she said in amazement.

"What do you mean, a village, Miss Know-It-All? That's not like any village I've ever seen. A village!" Lori was making a huge effort not to cry. She was shaking so hard Ari wondered if she'd shake herself right out of her riding boots.

Ari kept her voice gentle, the way she did when she handled a scared horse. "Those are buildings, don't you think?"

"With grass on the roofs? Don't be an idiot."

"Sure. You've seen pictures. Those are thatched roofs. You know, long grass that's dried and then put on top of a house to keep the rain out."

"I don't like it here. I want to go home. You take me home. Right now! If you don't, I'm going to tell Daddy to buy Chase and you'll never see him again."

Ari ignored her. "Where do you suppose we came out?" she asked thoughtfully.

"Came out? Came out?"

"Well, we're on the other side of the cave, aren't we?" Something Dr. Bohnes had told her about Glacier River came back to her now. "The land here folded and folded again when the glaciers came through millions of years ago."

Chase nodded. *The Gap.*

"So that's the Gap, Chase?"

"Stop that!" Lori shrieked. "Stop that right now!"

"Stop what?"

"Pretending that horse is talking to you!"

"Well, he is talking to me," Ari said reasonably.

"Don't be an idiot!"

Ari walked up to her horse and put her hands on either side of his muzzle. She pulled his head down and laid her cheek against the strange white scar on his forehead. It felt cool, cooler than the rest of him. "Can we go back the way we came?"

He nickered, low in his throat. *No.*

"Do you know where we are?"

On the other side of the Gap.

"Do you know what place this is?"

The wrinkles over his eyes grew deeper. *I . . .
I perhaps have dreamed of this place.*

"But you don't know where we are."

Before he could answer, Lori screamed, "Cut
it out, cut it out, CUT IT OUT!" She fairly danced
up and down in rage. "I want to go home RIGHT
NOW!"

"I don't know how to go home, and Chase
doesn't, either."

Lincoln whined, lay down on the grass, and
put his paws over his eyes. Did he understand what
she'd just said? Ari thought she truly would go crazy
if he started to talk to her, too. She found herself
hoping that the dog hadn't really understood what
she'd just said, but that he was tired. Or the sun was
hurting his eyes. Or something.

I want to go home, too.

Ari stared at him, her mouth open. *O-kay.*
The dog was talking, too. Lincoln's voice was different from Chase's. For one thing, he had an accent.
He sounded just like Mrs. Broadbent, the dressage
teacher. She came to the farm once a week to teach
first level to the riding students.

"Hel-lo," Lori said in an incredibly sarcastic
voice, jerking Ari's attention away from Lincoln's
newfound ability to chatter. "Earth to Ari. Let's get it

straight. You do know what's happened here, don't you?" The tears welled up in her eyes. "We've been abducted by aliens."

"We haven't been abducted by aliens. For one thing, the sun's in the same position it was when we fell through the cave."

"So?"

"So I think we're on the other side."

"The other side of what?"

"Of the farm. A different side. A side . . ." Ari hesitated, "that maybe was here all the time, but the glaciers folded it away. I mean, we can breathe the air and everything, Lori. And I've seen pictures of those thatched roofs in books. I know I have. If we were on another planet, everything would be weird."

"Oh?" Lori's eyebrows rose to her hairline. "You don't think this is weird? *Excuse* me, but this is weird enough for me, thank you very much. Now, let's get out of here."

Ari looked at Chase, standing regally alert, and at Lincoln, sitting majestically, if a little forlornly, on the grass. If they went home, would she be able to speak with them again?

"You do want to get out of here, don't you?" Lori's voice was quavering again.

"Sure. So let's go up to the village and ask how to get back."

"Are you crazy?"

"I don't think so."

130

Lori grabbed her by the shoulders and shook her. "What if they attack us?"

"Why should they?" Ari removed Lori's hands from her shoulders. "Here's what we'll do. Those trees are pretty thick. And the village is on the other side of the forest. So we'll go through the trees and wait until we see some people walking around and see how normal they look. If they look pretty normal, we'll . . ." Ari stopped. "We'll ask for the police station. Then we'll go to the police station and ask our way home."

"Finally, a plan that doesn't sound stupid." Lori folded her arms across her chest and tapped her foot.

"Good." Ari picked up Chase's lead line, whistled to Lincoln, and set off for the forest. "Are you coming?"

"I'm not walking all that way. I'm hot. I'm hungry. And I'm tired. I'm going to ride Chase."

Ari debated. She could drag Lori whining all the way through the woods, or she could put her on Chase and get some peace and quiet. She patted Chase's neck. "Do you mind?"

She sits like a sack of potatoes.

"Just don't dump her off, okay? We've had enough physical stuff this morning." She nodded to Lori. "He doesn't mind. Much. I'll give you a leg up." She crouched and cupped her hands together. Lori put her left foot into Ari's cupped hands. Ari counted "one, two, three" and on the count of three, pushed her hands up. Lori pushed off the ground with her right foot, then swung her right leg over Chase's back. The stallion snorted, tossed his head, and rolled his eyes. Ari raised her hand quietly, and Chase settled down with a grumble. Then Ari crouched down in front of Lincoln.

"You have a pretty good nose, boy?"

We collies have excellent noses.

"That's great. Can you lead us to the village? By scenting the people and . . ." Ari sighed. She'd missed breakfast this morning and she realized she was starved. "And the food?"

Of course. Lincoln's mental tone was lofty. *No problem at all. Of course,* he hesitated, *collies are not bloodhounds, you know.*

"I know."

Nor are we terriers. Terriers have excellent noses. However, a nose isn't everything, you know. There are more important issues for dogs than a great sense of smell. Beauty, for example. We collies are —

"Lincoln?"

— among the most handsome of breeds. . . .

"LINC!"

Yes?

Ari put her hands on her hips and regarded him with exasperated affection. My goodness. Who would have thought her beloved dog was as gabby as this? "Quiet, please. Just find us the village."

132

Right you are. He trotted ahead, plumed tail waving gaily. Ari walked behind him, not so much leading Chase as walking companionably side by side. They crossed the meadow. Linc's gold-and-black back almost disappeared in the tall grass, but the way was soft-going. The blades grew straight and tall. Despite how thick the grass was, it bent easily with their passage.

And the way was almost silent.

It was not as easy once they got to the woods. Inside the forest, the branches intertwined overhead to make a canopy that kept out the sun. The golden leaves held the light, much as a glass holds water.

Ari could see where they walked, but the close-growing trees made their forward progress almost blind. Thank goodness the branches started growing a third of the way up the trunks and the ground underfoot was thickly padded with leaves and not much else. At least they didn't have brush to wade through.

Lincoln's progress was erratic, just as it was when he and Ari went out for walks at home. He stopped and sniffed at piles of leaves, investigated mysterious holes, and occasionally marked the trunk of a tree with his scent, lifting one leg with an intent, faraway expression. The chief difference was that Ari heard all the dog's chatter in her mind, which was addressed as much to himself as to her:

Now that would be a woodchuck hole on the other side of the Gap, but Canis alone knows what animal den this would be. And that trail up the trunk, could have been a squirrel, but are there squirrels here on the other side of the Gap?

She became almost happy with the constant chatter the deeper they went into the woods. The leaves were darker here, the gold deepening to a dull brown. The forest was quiet and alternately dim and dark. Really quiet. And Lincoln's cheerful comments kept her mind from wondering what that dark hump really was at the foot of an especially large tree, or if she'd actually seen a shadow slip between the trunks of two slender saplings.

Lincoln came to an abrupt halt and growled. Ari froze in place. That was Lincoln's "stranger!" growl. The hair along the dog's creamy ruff rippled and stood up.

Chase stopped, ears forward. He curled his upper lip over his teeth.

Lori, a sob of fear in her throat, cried, "What! What is it?"

"Hush!" Ari strained her ears to hear. Flies. Black flies. And that horrible, dead animal odor that she'd smelled three times before.

Lincoln whirled to them, teeth snapping. *BACK! BEHIND THE TREE!*

To her astonishment, Ari heard Chase respond.

What? Chase demanded. *I hide from no thing nor beast, dog!*

Lincoln's tone was grim. *You'll hide from this! Quickly now!*

Ari couldn't stop to think about this new phenomenon. Her dog and her horse could talk to each other.

There was a quiver in the air, just like the beating of a drum. Ari counted under her breath, almost without realizing she was doing it. "One. Two. Three. Four."

"What is it?" Lori was so scared, she almost whispered with terror. Lincoln, cold determination in his eyes, nudged them behind the trunk of the largest tree near them.

The sound in the air grew closer:

"One. Two. Three. Four."

"Something's marching," Ari whispered. She looked up at Lori. The blond girl's face was white. Ari could hear the quick shallow breaths she took. "Easy, now," she said, just as she would to a frightened horse. "Deep breaths. Take very deep breaths."

"ONE! TWO! THREE! FOUR!"

There were voices in the beating of the air. Deep voices, many of them, and all of them marking time together.

Ari flattened herself against the tree, not daring to look around. Lori bent her head into Chase's mane and sobbed silently, her shoulders shaking.

Chase kept his head up, his nostrils flared. He was confused and angry. *Horses, milady. And yet, not horses.*

Ari was afraid to answer. Suddenly, Chase started forward, snorting. Lincoln flung himself in the way, pressing the great stallion's body out of sight of the oncoming marchers. Ari huddled between Chase's legs. The ground shook.

She had to see! Ari crawled forward, peering around the huge tree trunk, almost hidden in the leaves piled at its base.

The marchers came through the woods.

Ari stuffed her fist in her mouth to keep from screaming.

There were so many of them — perhaps a hundred. Each was coal black with red eyes, demon eyes. Each had an iron horn springing from the middle of its forehead.

Black unicorns.

An army of them.

They carried fear with them — and terror. It was in the air they breathed, the ground they marched upon. They passed the tree where the companions lay hidden, in pairs. Their flaming eyes stared straight ahead. Their coats were blacker than coal, blacker than the bottom of the night itself.

Ari's mouth was dry. Her breath was short. She may have fainted, just a little, from the utter horror of it.

When she opened her eyes, they were gone. The air was clean and sweet, the ground firm. It was as if they had never been.

"Lori?" Ari was surprised at how calm she sounded. "You okay?"

"I guess." Lori's voice was a mere squeak. "Did you look?"

"I looked."

"What *was* it?"

"Did you look?"

"No." Lori paused. "I mean, yes."

"Well, so you know what it was." Ari knew that Lori had been too scared to raise her head from Chase's mane. If she told Lori that'd she'd seen a herd of black and fire-eyed unicorns, evil in every step they took, the blond girl would dissolve in a sticky puddle of tears. And they'd never get out of this forest.

"I didn't exactly see, I guess. So what was it?"

"Just some . . . ah . . . bears."

"Bears!" Lori sat up with a squall.

Lincoln looked at Ari reproachfully, *Now you've done it. She won't stop shrieking until we get to the village.*

"BEARS!" Lori drummed her heels into Chase's sides. The stallion cocked his head at Ari. *May I dump her, milady?*

"You may not. We will just . . ." Ari sighed, "march on. Maybe she'll shut up when she sees we're close to safety."

137

None of them spoke again. The fear was still with them.

Half an hour later, Lincoln led them to the edge of the woods, and they gazed upon the village for the first time. Ari looked. She couldn't tell if it was safe or not. But there was a sign. And the sign said:

WELCOME TO BALINOR

Ari stopped. Stared. And a cold, cold wind blew over her heart. What was this? *What was this!*

More than a village lay ahead.

She took one step forward. Then another.

About the Author

Mary Stanton loves adventure. She has lived in Japan, Hawaii, and all over the United States. She has held many different jobs, including singing in a nightclub, working for an advertising agency, and writing for a TV cartoon series. Mary lives on a farm in upstate New York with some of the horses who inspire her to write adventure stories like the UNICORNS OF BALINOR.